Lock and Load

The dryness in Hanson's mouth increased as Berrenton took the patrol forward at a walk.

They advanced to within eighty or a hundred yards of the Indians. There was a shrill, ululating cry, and one of the savages stood, pointing back at the patrol.

Hanson cocked his revolver and was about to lay spurs to his horse when in front of them Indians began leaping into view. They popped up from the emptiness like so many jacks-in-the-box. Coming up from nowhere. Materializing in places Hanson would have sworn could not hide a field mouse. Indians. Armed and savage and terrifying. Turning now. Drawing their bows. Dozens of them. Perhaps scores.

Hanson trembled but not from fright. He was feeling the wild exhilaration of the will to battle, any nervousness forgotten now as he leaned eagerly forward with revolver extended toward the enemy.

Berrenton roared so loud it seemed he was trying to make up in voice volume what he lacked in numbers of troopers. "Charge!"

SIEGE

Frank Roderus

B
BERKLEY BOOKS, NEW YORK

SIEGE

A Berkley Book / published by arrangement with
the author

PRINTING HISTORY
Berkley edition / March 2003

For information address: The Berkley Publishing Group,
a division of Penguin Putnam Inc.,
375 Hudson Street, New York, New York 10014.

ISBN:0-425-18883-3

BERKLEY®
Berkley Books are published by The Berkley Publishing Group,
a division of Penguin Putnam Inc.,
375 Hudson Street, New York, New York 10014.
BERKLEY and the "B" design
are trademarks belonging to Penguin Putnam Inc.

PRINTED IN THE UNITED STATES OF AMERICA

10 9 8 7 6 5 4 3 2 1

✦ 1 ✦

DRY. BAKED. UGLY. He hadn't known there *was* country this miserable. Didn't much appreciate having to learn it now.

The view off in the distance was all dry and all brown. Yellow brown, red brown, gray brown, even a blackish brown on the mountain slopes. But all of it was brown.

The view close in wasn't much better. That was blue and brown. Brown horses. Blue uniforms. Both horses and men were streaked white with salt where old sweat dried.

Hanson didn't know about the others, but he was developing sores—galls, he supposed they would be considered—under his arms and in his groin. A bath would stop that. A few days of being clean would make them go away altogether. Hanson hadn't had a wash since they left Camp Lune six days ago. He hadn't had a proper tub bath since Fort Union way back in New Mexico, and that had been, what, well over a month now. Lune was too new and raw to afford luxuries. But a real bath would have been awfully nice.

He leaned back a little to stretch. Put his weight in the stirrups to lift a few inches off the saddle seat. Reached down to tug at his trousers in the faint hope of relieving the constant pinch. Lifted the black campaign hat—black!

of all stupidly hot colors, black—to let a little fresh air
reach his scalp. Once those small measures of relief were
concluded, he slumped as low in the saddle as he could
and encouraged the mindless ennui of a slow march to
claim him, eyes unfocused and mind emptied.

He was only dimly conscious of the sounds of the
march. The dull plop of shod hoofs on sunbaked soil. The
creak of leather and rattle of accouterments. The occasional whuff of a horse's snort or the liquid hiss of one
of them breaking wind. Six days they had been out, and
none of the eight troopers bothered making jokes any
longer when horse or man passed wind. Well, not unless
the transgression was thunderously magnificent. Excep-
tions might still be made in a case like that.

"Column halt." Corporal Berrenton spoke softly, barely
loud enough to be heard. On the parade ground or at drill,
Berrenton barked his commands sharp and loud, and woe
to the squad member who failed to instantly obey. Now
the corporal was as sun battered and weary as the rest of
them, and all the snap had been leeched from his voice.

The men drew to a straggling halt, all semblance of
formation abandoned.

"Dismount."

They did so, and Hanson's was not the only sigh uttered. It felt good to stand again, despite the twinges in
his knees. He stamped his feet and flexed his leg muscles
while he waited for the inevitable next command.

"Lead horses. Forward ho."

The manual said they should ride at a walk for forty
minutes, trot for ten, and walk dismounted for another ten.
The patrol hadn't ridden at the trot since the middle of
their fourth day out. The horses, not the best of mounts
to begin with, simply could not give that much.

The patrol was rationed for ten days, but grain was in
such short supply at Camp Lune that the mounts were
allotted a single quart of grain per day. They were sup-

posed to subsist on natural forage for the remainder of their needs. But there *was* no natural forage in this sere and arid land.

Without adequate grain and roughage, Berrenton had to adjust the patrol's movements to the horses' strength or bring his men back afoot. So they no longer moved at the trot and marched dismounted at least fifteen minutes out of every hour.

The men wanted more rest for themselves, too, but they did not get it. Because they were moving so slowly, the corporal would soon have to decide between shortening the range of assigned movement or lengthening the duration of the patrol. Either they disobeyed orders as to the area to be covered, or they went onto reduced rations. Neither prospect would be inviting to the man who was in charge. The men, naturally enough, hoped they would turn back toward Camp Lune just as quickly as possible. Hanson could understand both points of view but like the others would prefer a return to the meager comforts of the post.

Hanson smiled a little to himself. It seemed quite amazing that a cesspit like Lune could be viewed now as a haven of relief and comfort. It was all relative, wasn't it?

His expression hardened then as he made another comparison. Being here, on this patrol, in this desert, was considerably more comfortable than prison had been.

Bad as this was, it was better than the cells.

"Column halt.

"Mount.

"At the walk, forward ho."

No one else bothered to speak, but in the middle of the afternoon they were already glancing anxiously into the sky, willing the sun to more quickly fall so they could stop for the night.

✟ 2 ✟

"CORP'R'L."
    "Yo."
"Smoke, Corp'r'l. I see smoke over yonder."

Berrenton snatched his horse to a stop, forgetting to call out a command to halt. Private Thames's horse bumped into Berrenton's and then Private Joseph's horse walked into Thames's, resulting in a good bit of cussing and bellyaching. "Stop, goddammit, will you people stop," Berrenton yelped. The order might not have been military, but it worked. "Where?"

Private Beard, who'd made the claim, pointed off toward the northwest.

"That's not smoke, Beard. It's just dust raised by one of those whirlidoodles."

"No, Corp'r'l. Looks that way right this second 'cause the breeze has broke it up. Give it just a minute. You'll see."

Whether because he believed Beard or, more likely, because he wanted a moment of rest, Berrenton allowed the tiny column to wait for a puff of late-afternoon breeze to subside. The smoke, pale against the gray brown backdrop of a low bluff, solidified into a well-defined plume after a minute or so. "Well I'll be damn," Berrenton muttered.

"What d'you think it be, Corporal?" Vickers asked. "Injuns maybe?"

"Not Injuns, I don't think. They don't like to make so much smoke with their fires. Besides, rising tight like that, it looks like it's coming out of a chimney."

"There ain't no chimbleys out here, Corp'r'l."

"That's what I thought, too." Berrenton scratched the stubble from a week's growth of whiskers and said, "We'd best go see what it is."

"Could be trouble, Corporal."

"Yes, and it could be some ranch or farm, too. Whatever it is, the lieutenant will want to know about it. Finding out stuff, that's what we're here for."

"Jesus," Ragen mumbled. "I knew there had to be some reason why we're doing this shit."

"Yeah, and now you know what it is."

"Looks a long way off over there, Corp'r'l. We won't get there 'fore nightfall."

"That's all right. We can take a bearing on the mesa. We'll find it."

"What if it's Injuns, Corp'r'l?"

"I told you, goddammit, it ain't no Indians. Now let's move. No, wait a minute. Dismount yourselves. We'll lead off on foot. Let the animals rest a little and mayhap we can trot them some once the sun heat is gone. C'mon now, boys. Let's go see what there is to see over there."

"WELL I'LL BE a son of a bitch."

"Will be, Kelly? You passed being a sonuva-bitch last April."

"Quiet down, dammit," Berrenton grumbled in a voice too weary to carry any weight of conviction.

As his horse came to the top of this latest in an endless succession of rises and dips, Hanson, too, could see the reason for Kelly's blurted comment. A quarter mile or so before them lay buildings. Real, actual, honest-to-God buildings. Hell, they didn't have buildings yet at Camp Lune, Lune being one of the brand-new satellite posts thrown out to protect the California Road from Indian depredations and, not so coincidentally, from any Confederate incursions mounted out of Texas.

But these, these were genuine buildings all right, with doors and windows and lamplight showing inside two of the four or five buildings on the place. The place looked too big for any crop farm there could be in this dry country, so Hanson assumed it must be a livestock farm of the sort they called a *rancheria* or ranch out here.

"Halt," Berrenton said. "All right now. Dust yourselves off and sit tall. When we ride in there, you're going to look like soldiers of the Yew Ess Army. That includes you, Hanson. So straighten up, all of you. In column of twos now. Form on me. That's better. Close it up, Vickers. All right now. At the walk. Forward ho. Now at the trot . . . ho!"

They rode in, heads high and hoofs popping, sharp as if they were on parade. They had their pride, after all. Even Hanson.

✤ 4 ✤

GOD, IT WAS magnificent. Water. Running water. Well, sort of. There was a seep up on the side of the bluff and the farmer—rancher he would be called here—made a sort of miniature aqueduct using cactus stalks to carry the water down to his buildings. The fibrous pipe flowed into a basin from which household water could be dipped, then into a tank where the livestock were permitted to drink, spilling finally onto the ground where it was swallowed up within a distance of less than a rod.

But it was water, wonderful water, and the patrol was told they were welcome to bathe in the final outflow if they wished.

If they wished. If they wished? The evening bacon and hardtack hadn't had time to reach their bellies before they were all naked and standing in line to share a trickle of water no bigger around than a man's little finger.

Neckerchiefs served duty as washrags and, when wrung out, as towels, too. The mud they stood in was ignored. It would dry in due time and the dirt would brush off. For now they had water enough to wash in, and it was wonderful.

High spirits were the order of the day. Thames snapped Vickers on the bare rump with the wet end of his neck-

erchief, and Vickers let out a howl. Even so, Thames got
the worst of it. When he tried to dart away from Vickers's
angry retaliation, Thames slipped and went down full
length in the mud. And Vickers thumped him a good one
on the arm besides.

Even Corporal Berrenton looked pleased as Punch.

Hanson scrubbed the heat galls under his arms and in
his crotch and would have sworn he could feel the healing
before they so much as dried.

"Dead men."

The voice came out of the dark and shocked them into
immobility. It was a witch's voice, empty and cold. It was
the coldness of it much more than the fact that it was a
woman's voice that froze them in place.

"Dead," the hollow voice repeated. "All dead."

Hanson shivered.

"Dammit, Margaretta, you're supposed to be looking
after her."

A little girl of twelve or so came darting out of the
shadows, grasped the ghostly woman figure by the elbow,
and led her back toward the ranch house. If the child
found anything exceptional about there being eight naked
soldiers beside the stock tank, she did not show it.

"Sorry," the man said. His name was Hartford, Hard-
ford, something like that. From his place at the back of
the squad, Hanson hadn't caught the name for certain sure
when the rancher came out to welcome them.

"That's my missus. You mustn't mind her. She's bore
ten children and only Margaretta and my boy Jonathan
lived to see their fifth birthdays. When that last one died,
it done something to her mind. Every once in a while she
goes off. Gets to saying she sees the dead. She don't mean
nobody harm, and you needn't be scared. It's all those
dead children she has in mind, that's all."

Berrenton grabbed up his campaign hat to stand behind

while he assured the farmer it was perfectly all right, the men understood, there was no harm done.

The farmer—rancher, dammit, he was a rancher—went back inside, and the men exchanged some nervous laughter. But their jokes rang almost as hollow as the crazy woman's voice had been.

Perhaps they, as did Hanson, remembered that the woman's eerie voice spoke of dead men and not of dead children.

Hanson shivered again and finished his bath quickly and with no more joy.

✦ 5 ✦

SPIRITS WERE HIGH when they set out again in the thin light of dawn. The air was refreshingly cool, and their bellies were warm with coffee provided by Hartford. That turned out to be his name after all. Charles Hartford. He explained he didn't have enough supplies on hand to feed them all, but he gave them coffee and a dollop of molasses apiece to put into it and a couple quarts of mixed grain for each of the horses, so Hanson supposed they were feeling good this morning, too.

It was obvious that Corporal Berrenton was in a fine humor, for before they left, he actually told them what he intended.

"What we're gonna do," Berrenton explained, "is push as far to the west as we can get by this evenin' sundown. Then we turn south by east. Pick up the road somewhere west of the post and then follow it back. I figure that should bring us in just about on time. Maybe a day over, so if any of you want to be cautious an' hold back on your ration, that might be a good idea. But you do what you want. Just don't bellyache to me about it if you run out an' have to watch while everybody else eats."

"What about Injuns, Corp'r'l? Did you ast that man 'bout Injuns?"

"I asked him. He said they raid his livestock 'most every year but haven't bothered him otherwise. Said he hasn't seen hide nor hair of them yet this year an' hopes it stays that way."

"If there's no Injuns, Corp'r'l, why 're we still looking?"

Which seemed to use up the last of the corporal's good humor. "Because, goddammit, we was told to. Now let's mount up. At a walk now. Ho!" The corporal's voice had more bite to it today, and they all were sitting straighter after a night spent near the civilized comforts of running water and buildings that had roofs on them.

Half an hour later the irrepressible and sharp-eyed Private John Beard piped up again. "Corp'r'l."

"What is it this time?"

"I see some deer over there. They aren't so awful far off. Can we maybe shoot one an' have us some fresh meat?"

"Where the hell d'you see deer, Beard?"

"There, Corp'r'l. Right there." He pointed, everyone else quite naturally peering into the sparse, thorny, nearly leafless brush that popped up here and there on the arid landscape.

"Jesus Christ, Beard. Where the hell are you from?"

"Pittsburgh, Corp'r'l, but what's that got t' do with anything?"

"Because, goddammit, those are some of Mr. Hartford's goats, that's why. Don't you know what a deer looks like? Don't you?"

Beard didn't answer. Didn't have to, of course.

Even Hanson chuckled a little over that, and he found precious little in the way of camaraderie or agreement among the men of Berrenton's squad.

But to mistake a nanny goat for a whitetail deer . . . now that was pretty good. He wished he could write home and tell them about Beard and his mistake.

He wished he could.

✛ 6 ✛

BERRENTON LED THEM down a game trail into a wide gully or wash and stopped there. The bottom of the washout was a flat expanse of yellow red grit with a consistency somewhere between coarse sand and pea gravel.

"We'll lay over here for the nooning," the corporal said. "Won't likely find a better place." They had come perhaps fifteen miles, far short of the twenty they should have accomplished by midday, but one night of rest and decent fodder was not enough for the horses to fully recoup their strength.

"Everybody unsaddle. Then Joseph, you take the animals back up to where they might find themselves a mouthful of graze. Put them on hobbles not picket ropes so's they can forage a little. Everybody hear that? Hobbles.

"Hanson, I want you to dig a hole out there in the middle of this gully. They tell me there might could be water under the surface in these places, so let's see can we find some.

"The rest of you can gather up the driftwood that's laying here and there. We'll boil a little coffee to soak the weevil dens in."

Hanson unsaddled quickly, then stripped off his neckerchief and wet it from the canteen he'd freshly filled that morning at the Hartford ranch. He used the wet cloth to swab out the nostrils of his horse and dampen inside its lips.

"What the hell 're you doing that for?"

"Refreshes him. Almost as good as giving him a drink."

"What 're you, some kind of expert on this desert stuff?"

"Not no more than you are, Kelly, but I know a little about horses."

"You was cavalry before, wasn't you?"

Hanson hesitated for a moment. Then he nodded. "Yeah, I was cav before, too." He unclipped his hobbles from the cargo ring on his saddle and hung them from the headstall so Private Joseph would find them easily.

He removed the plate from his mess kit and used that as a shovel, kneeling in the middle of the wash in the midday heat, scooping gravel until pain shot like jagged lightning streaks through his shoulders and lower back and sweat ran stinging into his eyes.

The other squad members finished their tasks and got a fire started while Hanson dug. Hanson's was always the shittiest detail. He was used to it and anyway knew better than to complain. That would only make things worse.

"You haven't found water yet, Hanson?"

"No, Corporal."

"All right, goddammit. Come get you some coffee."

It hurt to stand up. He mopped his face with the now-dry neckerchief and tied the square of bright yellow cloth at his throat again. But damn any army that would make its men wear black hats and dark woolen blouses in country like this.

Hanson wiped his plate on his trouser leg and shoved

it back into the canvas mess kit bag, then pulled his cup from the same pouch.

He was helping himself to a cup of coffee when they heard the faint crackle of distant gunfire.

✢ 7 ✢

"WHAT THE HELL is that noise?" Ragen asked, coming to his feet so quickly he spilled hot coffee onto himself and yelped in pain.

Berrenton stood and cocked his head to listen. After a moment there was another hollow, muffled report, and then quickly again. The corporal shook his head. "Damn if I know."

"Sounds like somebody breaking wood."

"Naw, more like somebody's dropping something heavy."

Hanson gaped at them then blurted, "My God, haven't any of you people ever heard a skirmish before? Haven't any of you been in a battle? Surely you've been hunting and heard gunfire in the woods."

"Gunfire?" Berrenton repeated. "Are you sure about that, Hanson?"

"Hell yes, I'm sure, Corporal. Somebody is having a fight." While Hanson was speaking, there were two more of the dull reports, then a short pause and a third shot.

"Whoever it is, they aren't close. A mile, would you say?" Berrenton asked, fishing for Hanson's estimate as he clearly had no idea himself.

"Prob'ly more, Corporal. The sound is carrying down

this gully like its funneling through an ear trumpet. That fight could be two, three miles off."

Berrenton came to his feet and stared in the direction where Hanson was already looking.

The gully came down from the northwest where they could see several buttes and a low, barren mountain range.

There was one more gunshot and then silence.

The corporal did not look like a happy man. "I expect we'd best go see what this is about. Joseph, bring the horses back down. And see to your carbines, boys. Make sure your musket caps are fresh and your charges dry."

"Corp'r'l, what if it's Injuns out there?"

"Now, Beard, just what the hell d'you think we're here for? If there's white men out there, it's our job to protect them, and by God that's what we'll do."

"What if it's Injuns shooting at other Injuns, Corp'r'l?"

"Then we'll toss a coin to see which side we help and which we shoot. Does that make you feel better, Beard?"

"Yes, Corp'r'l. I mean . . . no, Corp'r'l."

Hanson dropped the breechblock of his Sharps and looked into the chamber to make sure the powder was dry and not caked. He pulled the underlever closed and threw away the percussion cap that had been in the carbine for the past several days. The old cap had been exposed to night air and could have been ruined, so he replaced it with a fresh cap.

Joseph brought the horses down, and the men began saddling them again after too short a rest.

Somewhere to the northwest there was another brief flurry of gunfire. Whoever was out there seemed to be holding his own.

✢ 8 ✢

THE WASH PETERED out after a little more than two
miles, ending about a quarter mile short of a loaf-
shaped mesa that had a vertical crack on its east wall like
some giant hand gave it a whack with an even more gi-
gantic ax. From the bottom of the wash they could see
nothing, but every few minutes they could hear a gunshot
coming from that direction.

"Halt. Stay on your horses. I'm gonna take a look,"
Berrenton told his men. The corporal stepped down and
handed his reins to Private Thames, then removed his kos-
suth hat and crept up the steep slope at the head of the
wash. He stayed there, crouching, for more than a minute,
then backed slowly down into the bottom and returned,
hat forgotten in his hand, carbine slapping at his right hip
where it dangled at the end of its keeper.

Berrenton grunted and paused for a moment in thought
before he spoke again. "I don't know how many people
are out there nor who they are, but I can see two bodies
lying in plain sight just this side of that cut in the side of
the butte, and there's movement at the bottom of it. It
looks to me like there's some people forted up in there.
Whites they must be. For sure the dead men are white.
You can tell that from the clothes.

"There's a bunch of Indians laying on the ground, holding them there like in a box trap. My guess is that the whites have guns and the Indians don't, but there's probably more of the Indians, so the whites can't get out, and the Indians can't get in. Got themselves a little siege going over there." The corporal put his hat back on and chewed at his lower lip for a moment. "It's our job to do something about this situation." Berrenton retrieved his reins and mounted, lifting his Sharps as he did so and dropping the barrel into the leather ring attached to his saddle so the weight of it would be carried there until he needed the weapon or was ready to dismount again.

Hanson nudged his horse around the others and approached Berrenton at the head of the tiny column. "Corporal, I don't mean t' intrude, but can I ask you a couple questions?"

Berrenton hesitated, then nodded. "All right, Hanson. I'll listen."

"The white men who're forted up over there. You didn't say anything about do they have horses or a wagon, a coach, what?"

Berrenton shook his head. "I didn't see anything like that. However they got there, I'd guess the Indians have it now."

"Which means they may have to walk out to safety. Some of us might have to as well, if we lose any mounts in the charge. There's always heavy losses among the horses in a mounted assault, Corporal. You can expect that. Some of us will be afoot, too."

"What is your point, Hanson?"

"No matter how few Indians there are, Corporal, we aren't likely to get them all, and we don't know how many others may be in the vicinity. A small group of men traveling on foot will be vulnerable to hit-and-run attacks once out into the open, and it's . . . what? . . . seventy-five miles or so back to Camp Lune? That would be the nearest source of relief, Corporal. On foot that would be at least three days' march. More if there are wounded."

Berrenton scowled but asked, "I see the problem, Hanson, but what are you suggesting?"

"My thought, Corporal, is that you should detail one man to ride back to tell Lieutenant Crowder and get a relief column started this way. No matter how things go over there when we hit those Indians, we're going to need help to get us and those civilians back to Camp Lune."

"Are you applying for that job, Hanson?"

He gave Berrenton a slow, level look and said, "No, Corporal, I am not."

Berrenton hesitated again, then asked, "You ever fight Indians before now, Hanson?"

"No, Corporal." He, too, hesitated, then added, "Only Yankee soldiers. But I've fought a power of you people, and I've made raids behind Yankee lines." He gave the corporal a grim but prideful smile. "Fought my way back out again every time but once, you see."

"Get back to your place in the column, Hanson."

"Yes, Corporal."

Berrenton once more dismounted and handed over his reins, again scrambled high enough on the end face to peer out onto the more-or-less level ground between the patrol and the mesa.

When he returned to the column and remounted, the corporal said, "Vickers, you're the lightest and the best rider; I want you to switch horses with Ragen." Ragen had the strongest horse among them, and Ragen pampered the animal outrageously. His mount was far and away in the best shape among the eight, probably the best in the entire troop.

"You'll carry a gallon of grain, your revolver, and your canteen. Nothing else. Nothing, you got that?"

"Yes, Corporal, but I don't have a gallon of grain."

"Collect some from the rest of us. We'll each give you

some if need be. Bury your carbine here. . . . We don't want some damned Indian finding it. . . . And share out your carbine ammunition to the boys you take grain from. I want you traveling light and fast. Not so fast you kill the horse, mind. At least not until you reach post. You're to tell the lieutenant it is my intention to break this siege and relieve whoever is trapped over there. Then we will march for Camp Lune at our best speed, if that is possible. If we believe the Indians will continue to present a threat, we will wait here for assistance from the troop. Is that clear, Vickers?"

"Yes, Corporal."

"Fine. We'll all dismount and see to our weapons and mounts while Ragen and Vickers make their switch."

There was a rattle and creak of saddles and equipment when the men complied.

Hanson glanced toward the sky. There were hours of daylight remaining. Plenty of time enough to fight. And to die. He wondered if the other six understood that or if they still felt the invulnerability of youth and ignorance.

Hanson himself felt tightness in his belly and a dryness in his mouth. He was afraid. Only a damned fool would not be. But he knew he would be steady when the time came. He hoped these Yankee soldiers would be, too. He had seen bluebellies turn and run like frightened sheep.

But then, truth to tell, he'd also seen Billy Yank walk steadfast and firm into the face of terrible musketry, pausing only to fall and to die. No, they weren't all cowards, these bluecoat soldiers.

He unfastened the flap over his holster and even though it probably was unnecessary replaced all six percussion caps on the handsome Colt revolver the Yankee army gave him. They issued good weapons, damn them, and had them in abundance to hand around.

Hanson took a deep breath and held it in for a moment,

then let it slowly out again. He swung onto his saddle without waiting to be told and laid the stubby, surprisingly heavy little Sharps across his pommel.

He was ready. He hoped the rest of them were as well.

✦ 9 ✦

BERRENTON WAITED UNTIL Vickers was out of sight on his way back to Camp Lune before he led the remainder of the patrol out of the wash to the desert above.

The place where the white men were forted up seemed terribly far away, even though it was not. Between the patrol and the trapped men they could see seven, eight, perhaps ten red Indians lying behind tufts of sage and greasewood, lying flat on the ground with no protection save the difficulty of anyone seeing them from a distance.

It surprised Hanson that the Indians were so very close to the rocks where he now saw a puff of gunsmoke. They were well under a hundred yards from the whites. Fifty or sixty would be more like it, he thought. He was accustomed to seeing men snipe at each other from much farther apart than that.

But then he had never seen a red Indian before this moment, much less seen how the savages fought.

He had, however, heard the bloodcurdling tales about their cruelty in the way they treated anyone they captured alive. The stories were enough to turn a hungry man's stomach and make him walk away from food. Slashing, jabbing, burning, even skinning a man while yet he was alive . . . the tales were too much to contemplate.

Still they could see only a handful of the Indians. A mounted patrol armed with revolvers should be able to rout them and break the siege in a single charge. The only weapons Hanson could see were bows and arrows and spears. Good Lord! Spears. He'd thought civilization much too thoroughly advanced for there to still be spears actively employed in warfare. But then these were, after all, a primitive foe as well as a savage one.

The dryness in Hanson's mouth increased as Berrenton motioned for the squad to come into a line abreast.

Again using his hand to signal so they would make as little noise as possible and come near the Indians before launching the charge undetected, Berrenton took the patrol forward at a walk.

"Draw pistols," he said in a low voice. The corporal sounded calm and sure of both himself and his men. That was much to the good, Hanson thought. The corporal was not blooded, but he seemed staunch enough, and that was important. Men would follow a good leader into the jaws of Hell itself and not flinch away. Hanson had seen that more times than he'd ever wanted. He hoped he would see it now as well.

They advanced almost half the distance to the bluff, to within eighty or a hundred yards of the nearest of the Indians, before in front of them there was a shrill, ululating cry, and one of the savages stood, pointing back at the patrol.

"All right, boys, let's have at them," Berrenton roared so loud it seemed he was trying to make up in voice volume what he lacked in number of troopers.

Hanson cocked his revolver and was about to lay spurs to his horse when in front of them Indians began leaping into view. They popped up from the emptiness like so many jacks-in-the-box. Coming up from nowhere. Materializing in places Hanson would have sworn could not hide a field mouse. Indians. Armed and savage and terrifying. Turning now. Drawing their bows. Dozens of them. Perhaps scores.

Hanson trembled but not from fright. He was feeling the wild exhilaration of the will to battle, any nervousness forgotten now as he leaned eagerly forward with revolver extended toward the enemy.

"Charge!"

NOTHING, NOT ANYTHING on all this earth, could be half so exhilarating as the feel and the sound of a cavalry charge. Hanson's heart raced, and his belly was at the same time both hollow and heavy. His breath rushed madly in and out, and his vision was unnaturally sharp. His senses quickened so that time itself seemed to stand still, and he was acutely conscious of the feel of the horse beneath him, the powerful bunch and surge of a thousand pounds of muscle launched full tilt toward the enemy.

Hanson wanted nothing so much now as to close the fight. He leaned far forward and extended his revolver toward the savages ahead, not so he would become a smaller target as he approached but in an attempt to get that much nearer to them just that much sooner.

He felt something pulse and grow within his chest. Fear, yes, but joy even more. A fierce and terrible joy. Power and mastery and the lust to kill and conquer.

Without bidding it, he tilted his head back and loosed the high, ululating cry that was the rebel yell. The sound of it blended with the thunder of pounding hoofs and rode ahead of them.

What a mounted charge must look like to an enemy on foot, soldier or savage, either one, was something Hanson

could scarcely imagine and hoped he would never himself
have to experience.

He watched with what was almost detachment as the
Indians turned to face the wildly oncoming charge. They
darted and swarmed, some dashing out of the way but
others standing to fight.

Standing. God! There were not the handful that had
been seen from the head of the washout. There were dozens of them popping up from the grass like so many prai-
rie dogs. Jumping into view, then disappearing again.

Thin, black splinters began to rise into the air in grace-
ful arcs. It took Hanson a moment to realize that these
were arrows. The Indians were shooting at them, creating
a curtain of falling arrows that the patrol charged into and
through.

It was a soundless volley and perhaps for that reason
seemed to him more interesting than threatening.

An arrow passed to the left of his horse's head, and
others dropped in front or behind as if falling from the
sky.

The squad charged through the lethal hail and inside
the arc, and now the Indians aimed in flatter, more inti-
mate trajectory, their arrows slicing at them with wicked
speed. Hanson could see them come, but too quick to react
to. One passed so close to his extended hand that he
thought it would lodge in the barrel of his Colt, but it
went by without noise or at least without sound loud
enough to be heard above the pounding of the horses and
Hanson's own wild war cries.

It took what must have been seconds to close with the
enemy. The time felt like minutes.

Then they were within range.

Hanson snapped his first shot at an Indian wearing
nothing but a breechclout and a necklace of shells—an
incongruous sight in the desert but he was sure of what
he saw—and missed.

A young warrior who looked barely into his teens leaped at Hanson's bridle, probably attempting to snatch the horse's head around and bring down both beast and man. Hanson shot him in the face and thundered past before the boy had time to fall.

Hanson fired again. Missed his man. Turned in the saddle and shot a savage with a drawn bow. The ball took effect somewhere in the man's torso, and he doubled over, his arrow discharging harmlessly into the ground at his feet.

Hanson fired his fifth and final shot at a target that materialized beside his left stirrup, and he had no idea if he hit that one or not.

He knew good and well the sixth chamber would not fire but thumbed the hammer and triggered the revolver anyway, the hammer falling onto an empty nipple. The revolvers were called six-shooters, but only five could be fired at a time. The recoil of the first shot invariably threw the brass percussion cap off the sixth nipple, where the loading cutout left it exposed. The others were held in place by the recoil shield, but the sixth cap always dropped off, no matter how a man tried to crimp the thin foil onto the steel nipple.

By then, the patrol had cut through the line of savages anyway. Hanson yanked his horse to a sliding stop and wheeled about, ready to exchange the empty revolver for his carbine and charge again, wishing for a saber for the close-in fighting. The Yankee cav didn't carry them out here, although they certainly were using them back East.

What this fight needed, though, was another charge. Back into the Indians's line, then turn and ride down it to roll them up and put them into rout.

Hanson swiveled about in his saddle, seeking Berrenton's orders to assemble and charge. Instead, he saw the rest of the squad finish their dash across the barren desert floor and into the sheltering cut where the white defenders crouched.

Hanson was alone in front of the Indian lines.

A cold knot filled his belly and his throat, but the blood lust was still on him.

He stood in his stirrups and shrieked the rebel yell again, brandishing the empty Colt defiantly.

Then common sense and stark fear overtook those impulses.

He yanked his horse's head around and stabbed his spurs into its flanks as a hail of arrows streamed past.

He was still yelling, though, when he reached friendly forces and leaped a low embrasure in the wall of stone the defenders must have thrown together.

Hanson was grinning and still full of fight when he threw himself off the horse and turned to face the Indians with his carbine.

God! There really was nothing, nothing remotely so wild and wonderful as a cavalry charge.

✦ 11 ✦

RAGEN WAS STANDING next to him when Hanson turned loose of the horse and turned to face the Indians. The young trooper, a farm boy from Vermont, gave him a pale, stricken look. "Jesus God, Hanson, you really are a reb." He shook his head and shuddered. "That yell . . . I never heard nothing like that before. Ever."

Judging from the tone of Ragen's voice, he was more afraid of Hanson now than he was of the Indians. But then, the Indians were out there on the other side of the stone defenses, whereas now the always-silent former Confederate had shown himself to be a warrior. And Ragen quite obviously was not accustomed to war or warriors.

Hanson ignored the comment—the fact that he'd paroled out of prison and agreed to wear damnyankee blue for duty in the West was no secret to any of them—and trotted over to the wall to peer out toward this enemy.

There was not an Indian in sight. Not one.

A hand and arm appeared briefly over on the right, the hand holding a drawn bow. The arrow was launched blindly, soaring high in the air and falling almost straight down to land with a faint thump a good ten yards in front of the white men's defensive position.

Not all of the Indian arrows missed, however.

Hanson slid down behind a boulder—although small good that would do to protect a man from arrows raining down from overhead—and took a few moments to assess what it was the patrol had ridden into.

What he saw was not heartening. There were, or anyway had been, an even dozen whites trapped here by the Indians. The men were civilians, burly and bearded. Hanson might have taken them to be teamsters caught out while hauling freight, except there were neither horses nor wagons anywhere in view. The men seemed to have arrived at this point pushing a pair of sturdily built handcarts. Nearly empty carts at that, he noticed. Each cart now held only a very few burlap sacks tumbled inside. Blankets and some cooking utensils now spread out on the ground would have been the rest of the load carried in the carts.

Handcarts! It was a poor man who would choose to travel country like this with nothing but a handcart and shank's mare.

A dozen men traveling on foot. When they got here. Now three were laid out toward the back of the rock-walled enclosure with bits of brush placed over them to keep the birds from pecking out their eyes and other choice bits. From where he was now, Hanson could not see what killed the men.

An arrow hit a boulder nearby and clattered noisily to the ground.

It was not difficult to guess why those three were dead.

One of the remaining nine was off to one side talking with Berrenton. Which was just as well. Hanson thought he probably ought to speak with the corporal but was too angry right now for that to be a good idea. Berrenton was brave enough, but the corporal had thrown away their opportunity to break the Indian attack and roll up their line.

Hanson grunted softly to himself and told himself to

calm down. It was too late to change what the squad leader had already done. And months ago, when he first accepted parole, Hanson vowed he would do whatever he was told, anything he was told, and remain aloof from these blue-clad troopers.

Of course his life was on the line here now, too. It wasn't just the Yanks.

And, dammit, not all the damnyankee soldiers were sons of bitches. They were kids, farm boys most of them, who could be expected to have at least some acquaintance with horses. The troopers were raw and inexperienced, but they seemed willing enough to face the dangers that came their way. They complained, of course. But hell, all soldiers complain, complaint being one of the few outlets of expression open to them.

Hanson really did not know what the hell to think about these young Yankee soldiers, all the more so now they were in this trap with wild savages outside.

Two or three more arrows thumped harmlessly to earth, and a few feet away, Private Nathan Joseph cringed, ducking low behind a rock that could not possibly protect him from missiles falling out of the sky.

Hanson walked away from the wall to have a look around and see what it was they had to work with here.

It wasn't much. The area where they'd taken refuge from the savages was roughly—very roughly—triangular in shape, much like the hole left behind when a wedge of cheese was sliced out of a chunk. Rocks large and small were scattered in and in front of this depression, presumably the material that had somehow fallen away from the mesa behind them.

The wedge-shaped cut was about forty feet across by thirty feet deep. At the back there were walls too sheer to scramble up, effectively blocking any idea of an escape via simple retreat.

Hanson carefully inspected what he could see of the

top of those walls. He guessed the top of the mesa was eighty or so feet above the floor where civilians and troopers were sheltering now. God help them all, he thought, if the Indians found a way to get up there. From the top, the savages would be able to direct aimed fire onto their victims, and there would be no hiding from it.

The civilians had already turned the small area into a sort of fortress, collecting loose stone and piling it to fashion a wall high enough for a man to crouch or sit behind in relative safety.

But only relative. There were the three dead men lying at the back of the wedge to testify to that, and Hanson saw now that four of the nine living civilians were bandaged, three of them having been wounded in the legs and one—judging only by the way the wound was bound— he must have been hit in the armpit. Hanson wondered how in hell a man got himself wounded in the armpit. Still, he'd seen stranger wounds than that. Just not very often.

The civilians had only three rifles and a shotgun among them, and he could also see one man with a pepperbox revolving barrel pistol in his hand. Fat lot of good that was apt to do as most of the pepperboxes came in pipsqueak calibers to keep their weight from becoming unwieldy, .28 to .31 caliber being the general sizes preferred.

There had been twelve men traveling with handcarts and so very poorly armed. Stupid, Hanson thought. Amazing in their stupidity.

He sighed. In perfect fairness, he would have to admit that the stupid civilians found themselves now in the exact same position as the trained and intrepid cavalry troopers.

Some days you just can't win for losing.

Hanson leaned against one of the large boulders that, lying naturally in place at the mouth of the wedge, had been used to anchor the defensive wall. He laid his carbine on top of the boulder and began carefully reloading the five empty chambers in his Colt cylinder, biting the end off the paper cartridge and using the built-in ram to secure each in place before fitting caps onto the nipples. That was a chore much easier done now than it would have been while mounted on a running horse.

Funny thing though. At this moment, Hanson really would rather be on the back of a running horse.

✠ 12 ✠

"HANSON!"

"Yes, Corporal."

"Come over here."

Hanson joined Berrenton and the civilian, a bearded man with a large belly and unkempt hair. The civilian wore bib overalls and a red flannel shirt. "You don't happen to speak German do you, Hanson?"

"No, Corporal."

Berrenton grunted. "Mine is poor, dammit." He looked at the civilian and said something, the words slow and halting and entirely incomprehensible to Hanson. When he turned his attention back to Hanson, he said, "These men claim to be saints. Crazy sons of bitches, I guess."

"Maybe not, Corporal. They could be Mormons. Lots of them in this country, or so I'm told. Never saw one my own self before, but these could be some. Back before," he couldn't help saying, "before the War for Southern Independence, that is, I read about the Mormons recruiting from all over. Looking for converts and promising free land someplace called Deseret. Come to think of it, that would explain the handcart, too. Thousands of them came over on ships from Europe. They were given handcarts and a little food and told to walk west to Deseret. I'm not sure where that's supposed to be, but it's someplace out West here."

"Yeah, that makes sense. This bunch came from Switzerland. The gent in charge of them is Mr. Heuer."

The Swiss brightened at the sound of his name and bowed repeatedly in Hanson's direction. He said something in German, and Berrenton explained, "They left the other saints and came south looking for gold. Said they heard America was knee deep in gold free for the taking."

"I expect they've learned better than that," Hanson said.

"You'd think so, but Herr Heuer claims they found a jim-dandy of a vein. Helluva strike, I guess. Then the Injuns jumped them. They don't know why. Just hate all white men, could be. But they came to fight with not a word of talk beforehand. Killed one man right off. Heuer and them fought the Injuns off and buried their dead man. Thought it was all over, so they went back to digging gold. Then here come the Injuns again.

"Damned red devils kept attacking time and again. Killed a couple more of them. Eventually the ones that were left got the hint and gave up their mining. Covered over the entrance so nobody else would likely find it and packed up. They left the gold buried there at the mine, wherever that is, and lit out fast as they could go. Which wasn't all that fast, seeing as they were afoot. Injuns followed after them and caught up with them on the flat out yonder. They been holed up here three days and are most out of water, only have a little powder and ball left."

"Just between you and me, Corporal, why is it that you're telling me all this? I'm just another trooper following orders."

"I'll tell you why, Hanson. You're the only man in this crowd who's been in combat before. I hate that. Could've been my brother or one of my uncles you've tried to kill in the past. But the point is, you've been there. You know something about it. I saw how you acted out there with

those Injuns. You wanted to take it to them. I could see
that. If I'd known . . . Never mind. We're here now. We're
going to make the best of it and do what we can to handle
this situation until the relief column arrives. In the mean-
time, Hanson, I want to get your opinion about some
things. I'm not turning this command over to you, mind.
You're just another trooper, and you'll take orders like
everybody else. But I want your advice if you're willing
to give it."

The Swiss asked something, and Berrenton and he
spent some considerable amount of time talking back and
forth between them.

Hanson was pleased enough for that respite because he
had no idea what he ought to tell Berrenton in response
to that last comment.

✦ 13 ✦

HANSON LEANED AGAINST the boulder trying to work out whether it was already too late to go out there and rout the Indians with a charge from horseback. Seven horses just might be enough, he was thinking. If they could rush out in tight formation and charge the left, then wheel and take it along the line . . . Damn, he wished they had sabers with them.

Revolvers are fine. Wonderful even. But once they're empty, they're useless. Not even heavy enough to make good cudgels.

Still and all . . .

He motioned for Berrenton to join him, forgetting for the moment that it would be proper for him to go to the corporal instead of expecting it to be the other way around.

"What are you thinking, Hanson?" Berrenton asked as he, too, looked over the top of the boulder toward what appeared to be empty, lifeless desert scrub in front of them.

Over to the right, two bows briefly appeared, and two arrows arced high, then fell. One clattered harmlessly against the stone wall. The other lodged deep in the rump of Michael Kelly's horse.

The animal grunted and tried to bolt away from the pain, wheeling and making an escape over the low wall. It hadn't run fifty yards before an Indian rose up in front of it to grab its trailing reins, then drop out of sight once more with the wounded horse secured.

Kelly cursed and loosed a shot in the direction of the Indian, taking his aim by the place where the reins disappeared from view. There was a yelp of pain.

"Got the son of a bitch," Kelly exulted.

"Maybe," Hanson said. "Good way to keep a man from shooting at you the second time is to make him think he's already killed you." He smiled. "Let's see did you get him or not."

Hanson thumbed back the hammer of his Sharps and took a bead on the same approximate place where Kelly had shot. He tripped the trigger and kept his eyes on the spot where he'd been aiming, unmindful of the recoil from the relatively mild powder charge.

Through a thin haze of smoke, he caught a glimpse of someone or something jerking into view and then dropping to cover again.

Kelly fired again while Hanson reloaded. This time there was no response from the Indian, and a moment later Kelly's horse began to drift away, limping badly and with the arrow standing upright in its nigh haunch.

Kelly aimed into the grass again, but Hanson told him, "You already got that one, Kelly, and we don't have so much ammunition with us that we should ought to waste any. It'll be days before relief gets here."

The trooper dropped his carbine and jumped to his feet. "I don't see no stripes on your sleeve, you grayback son of a bitch."

"Shut up," Berrenton snapped. "Hanson is right. There's no point wasting a ball on a dead Injun." He raised his voice. "Everybody hear that? We weren't issued but forty rounds apiece, and those forty have to last us until the lieutenant gets here with the rest of the troop. So don't shoot unless you're sure of your aim. We can't be wasteful."

Hanson thought most of the squad would do all right. Like Kelly. The mick had himself a temper, but he hadn't hesitated to shoot. Joseph, on the other hand, was trying to hide the fact that he was so scared he was crying and probably couldn't have fired an aimed shot if his life depended on it . . . which it damn well might.

It was a funny thing about that. There were men who would ride and run and cuss and spit and talk one helluva scrap, but when it came down to pulling a trigger and sending a bullet into another man's gut, they just couldn't bring themselves to do it. Hanson had seen more of that kind than he wanted, even in Confederate gray.

Then there were those like Kelly who could be counted on to be there when it was the other side doing the shooting, stand there and shoot back and spit in the bastards' faces when they got to where that was all they had left.

What Hanson decided now that they were down to only six horses among the seven troopers was to suggest to Berrenton that he put Kelly up on Joseph's horse for their second charge. Joseph could stay back and give covering fire. Be told to shoot, anyhow. When the time came he maybe would or maybe wouldn't, but better to have him here than out there where things were likely to be hot.

They could all leave their carbines here, too. Let the Swiss use them while the squad made their attack with revolvers. One of them—Hanson expected to nominate himself—could carry Joseph's revolver to use when his first ran dry.

Hanson opened his mouth to suggest his plan to Berrenton but never got the words out.

An arrow came whizzing over the stone parapet with a rapid, fluttering sound and buried itself feather deep in Michael Kelly's chest.

"Jesus!" Kelly uttered, looking down at what little of the arrow protruded from his blouse. His expression was more surprised than pained. What Kelly mercifully could not see was the blood-smeared flint arrowhead and eight or ten inches of shaft sticking out his back.

"Oh, God," someone mumbled.

Kelly kept looking at the feathers—pigeon feathers, Hanson thought—until his knees became weak and he sagged slowly to the ground.

Joseph was weeping openly now. The squad members, save Hanson and the corporal, rushed to gather beside Kelly to give what comfort they could while he died. The Swiss seemed indifferent.

Six men, Hanson was thinking. Six horses.

He did not know if that would be enough to do what needed to be done.

✢ 14 ✢

"No," BERRENTON SNAPPED without hesitation. "I will not take this squad outside the protection of this position. Your idea exposes all of us to direct fire. I won't do it."

"It's a chance, Corporal. It takes the fight to them. Gives us a chance to break the siege. But we have to do it quick while we still have enough men and mounts to have any hope at all."

"I already told you, Hanson. My answer is no and it will remain no. We can wait here until the relief column arrives. I'll not jeopardize this command like you suggest. I just won't do it." Berrenton turned and walked back to the Swiss.

A pair of arrows fell out of the sky, embedding themselves into the gravel between the makeshift redoubt and the clutch of horses who were at the back wall picking at the dry, windblown brush there in search of nourishment.

One of the Swiss fired at a target Hanson could not see. The Swiss men's rifles were old but not rusted. Army muskets of a type that wouldn't have been in service for twenty or thirty years, he guessed. Old enough that the locks were fired by flint instead of caps. Cheap goods, he thought, and not always reliable to ignite. These had bores

larger than the current standard .58 caliber, but he did not
think they were as large as the .72 caliber musket his
grandpap had carried during the first rebellion against tyr-
anny.

Not that it mattered.

Not ten yards in front of the wall, an Indian jumped
into view and rushed forward, a lone, near-naked man
charging a fortified position with nothing but a stone-
headed club for a weapon. The man was crazy, but God
he had balls.

Thames fired his carbine. The bullet knocked the Indian's leg out from under him, and he hit the ground
where Beard finished him off with a bullet in the side of
his head. It was messy.

In a way, Hanson was glad for that. His reaction had
nothing to do with that Indian nor with Indians in general.
He wanted these Yankee boys to see the way things really
were, without all the drums and the bugles and the ex-
pectations of glory. He wanted them to see that it was a
living man's gut spilled out onto the ground steaming in
the chill morning air or—like now—a skull burst apart
and sticky gray brains scattered across the ground like
garbage flung out for hogs to eat.

It would be good for them to see and to know so they
could get over any notions of brave fancy and get down
to the very serious business of killing the other guy before
he could kill you.

They all saw. Except Joseph, who lay huddled at the
base of the biggest boulder and seemed only to be seeing
demons.

"Beard, Thames, that was good shooting," he said in a
strong voice that should carry to all of them.

The Swiss with the shotgun fired, a cloud of smoke
rising into the still air and hanging above him.

A small swarm of arrows, three, four, maybe more of
them, came whizzing into the smoke in response, but by

then the Swiss had ducked below the top of the rock wall and was taking his time about carefully reloading.

Hanson heard a sharp curse from Berrenton and turned to see that one of those arrows struck the ground and deflected into the off foreleg of Berrenton's horse.

Hanson wanted to cuss, too. Five horses now. Even if Berrenton changed his mind about trying to break the siege . . . not that he supposed it mattered.

Out in front of them he caught a glimpse of something dark moving in the scrub. Hanson brought his carbine to bear and fired. The dark object that could have been an Indian's head disappeared, but he had no idea if he'd hit anything or not.

This was not exactly the sort of fighting he was used to. At least the sonuvabitch Yankees stood upright when they shot at you.

He quickly reloaded the Sharps and waited for another target to present itself.

✦ 15 ✦

"ALL RIGHT EVERYBODY, listen up. Herr Heuer tells me that him and his people have a problem. They're short of water. We aren't. We have plenty enough to last us until the relief gets here, so what I want us to do is to share with the civilians."

There was a general round of groaning and murmuring, but none of the troopers actually spoke up in objection. The corporal went on, "The deal is this. The Swiss have some stuff, I suppose you'd call it desiccated soup. You put it in water and boil it, and it makes a hot soup. He says it's pretty good. He also says if we want to share enough water to make it, they'll share their soup with us. So anybody who wants to stick with hard cracker and bacon can do that. But anybody who wants to contribute water for the soup will get some of that. Personally, I'm gonna have myself some soup for supper tonight."

While Berrenton was having that conversation, one of the Swiss, a blond man with sun-reddened skin and a makeshift bandage on his left hand, was using a magnifying glass to start a fire courtesy of the afternoon sun.

There was enough dry brush inside the wall to provide wood for cooking but not enough to keep a fire going constantly, hence the need to start the fire afresh whenever they needed one.

"Make up your minds about the soup, boys," Berrenton prompted.

Each man in the squad fetched out his canteen and contributed to the soup pot.

Except Hanson.

✢ 16 ✢

I F IT HADN'T been for the spicy sauce of danger that lay inside the makeshift redoubt as silent as a snake, the experience would have been quite boring.

This form of siege was not at all what Hanson would have imagined, and he suspected the same would hold true with each of the other men as well.

His vision of battling wild Indians, influenced by drawings in books and magazines and newspaper accounts, was of racing horses and hordes of feathered savages wielding clubs and axes and bows. Well, the bows were certainly out there. The clubs and the axes might well be also. But the Indians themselves were an invisible presence. He had seen them clearly only during their initial charge into the fortification. Since that time they were represented mostly by arrows that flew from nowhere and landed willy-nilly, with no regard for accuracy.

That might have been considered a cowardly way for men to fight, save for one thing. It presented a threat to the enemy with virtually no danger to the one doing the shooting.

Most of the arrows—and in truth there were not all that many fired—landed harmless in the ground or bounced off stone, their tips shattered and shafts splintered.

While the others ate, Hanson saw to the horses, then picked up several of the expended arrows. He had never seen a real Indian arrow before and was fascinated by them.

He had expected . . . he didn't know what he expected. Something more cunningly fashioned than this, he supposed. These arrows were crude. Very.

They were not particularly long. History spoke of English archers as the acme of the bowman in warfare, using their man-tall yew bows to fling arrows more than a yard long.

Hanson had no real knowledge of the bows the Indians crafted except that they were short and puny-looking things. But he could see here that their arrows were short, almost stubby things and seemed to be whatever length the available wood allowed. Under two feet and some a mere foot and a half long.

The shafts were reasonably straight. But not perfectly so. And the feathers were merely tied onto the butt ends of the shafts with gut or sinew.

The arrowheads seemed to have been crafted from whatever material came to hand. Most that he saw here were flint knapped into a tiny knife point no larger than a fingernail. Much, much smaller than he'd envisioned. Some were bits of light bone, taken from some bird, he suspected, and sharpened by abrasion. Wild savages would not have grindstones, he thought, but this sort of shaping could be done using any rough stone to rub against.

He found it curious that on the arrows he picked up and examined here not a single one had a metal head, even though the Indians in the grass out there had at least some muskets and their drab, ragged costumes reflected at least a few metal adornments.

He hadn't seen a single feathered headdress out there. Not one. The savages were bareheaded for the most part although with perhaps a cloth wrapped around their heads to contain their hair. Or to keep sweat from their eyes? He wondered if Indians sweat. It was something he'd not questioned before. But now that he thought about it, he supposed that they must, even though that seemed so . . . ordinary. His image of Indians was as something other than fully human, fully normal.

Another arrow lofted over the stone parapet. It grazed off the hip of John Beard's leggy brown horse, doing no serious harm but causing a momentary commotion among the animals.

Hanson dug at the base of the cliff behind them to find a handful of loose dirt that was free of gravel, then applied that to the small cut on the horse to clot the blood and stop it from flowing.

He brushed his hands clean on the seat of his britches and knelt to rummage through his gear for a hardtack biscuit.

Suppertime in the desert twilight, the sky clear and in the distance a sound of . . . quail? He thought so. Quail and mourning doves.

The bird sounds brought memories rushing into his head so strong and painful they brought tears to his eyes. A surge of anger drove those memories away, and he clenched his jaw and steeled himself against any recall of those things, those places, those people. He had no time now for any of that. He wedged a small corner of the thick, doughy cracker between his teeth and concentrated solely on trying to gnaw a few flakes of the material free so he could moisten it in his mouth and eat it. Although God alone knew why any mortal man would voluntarily subject himself to the misery of hardtack.

✦ 17 ✦

"THEY'RE COMING!" AT the same time Ragen shouted, one of the Swiss screamed something in German as well.

Soup cups fell and curses flew as the men leaped to the wall with their weapons.

Six, seven, maybe as many as nine of the savages were running toward the wall with clubs waving and hoarse shrieks. They were still sixty or seventy yards away but coming fast and furious.

The defenders' carbines and rifles barked, and every one of the Indians dropped facedown in the dirt.

"Oh, shit!" Hanson muttered as he yanked back the hammer of his Sharps.

From hiding places much closer to the fortification, four more Indians suddenly appeared. They obviously were waiting there by prearrangement, ready to complete the charge as soon as the defenders' weapons were empty.

Hanson snapped a shot at the first to come into his sights. His ball struck the savage squarely on the breastbone, shattering a ladderlike bone decoration that hung there and sending painted splinters flying. The Indian collapsed onto the ground and lay there as motionless as the earth that cradled him.

From his right, Hanson heard the bellow of a shotgun, and another of the Indians was spun around, his left side a red mass of torn flesh. The remaining two grabbed their wounded comrade under the arms and ran back toward the others.

At least two of the troopers had their carbines reloaded by that time. Ragen and Thames. They stood behind the wall watching the Indians carry the wounded one toward safety.

"Shoot, dammit. Shoot the sons of bitches!" Hanson shouted, his fingers flying as he shoved a paper cartridge into the breech of the Sharps and tried to fumble a fresh cap onto the nipple.

The Indians reached a point of relative safety and dropped out of sight in the thin grass that grew out there.

"You could've shot them," Hanson accused.

"They were retreating," Berrenton put in. The corporal stepped between Hanson and Thames, one hand held out as if to stop Hanson from advancing toward the bluecoat soldier.

"Yes, and now they're alive to come at us again."

"But they were running away," Ragen said.

"Goddammit, haven't you dumb sons of bitches figured this out yet? There's no rules in war save one, and that's to make sure it's the other man that dies, not you. You let those Indians live. Next time you could die because of not shooting just now." He glared at the men behind the wall, Yankee and Swiss alike. With his voice raised, Hanson said, "I didn't come here with a mind to die. I intend to live. And if that means you and me got to kill every red sonuvabitch in this territory in order for us to get out of here alive, then that's what we'd better do. So forget about rules. Forget about glory. Forget everything you thought you ever knew about how battles ought to be conducted. It all comes down to this. You got to kill and keep on killing till there's nobody left out there you have to kill."

Hanson was breathing heavily, his heart pounding in his anger. He tried to calm himself and looked at Berrenton. "Sorry, Corporal." But he wasn't. Not really.

He wouldn't have thought it possible out here so far from green vegetation or much of anything living, but from somewhere in this sunbaked desert, flies appeared. A few at first and then more and more of them. They gathered to feast on the blood spilled onto the dirt and to crawl over the eyes and into the mouth of the Indian that Hanson had killed.

Hanson had come to hate flies. Hated the sight of them so bad that the hating curdled his stomach and gave him the shakes. At least that was what he believed was making him tremble so badly now.

He lay his carbine loaded and ready atop the wall and tried once more to attack the square of hardtack he'd been chewing on when the attack came. But neither his hands nor his jaw muscles were working normally at the moment, and it was some time before he was calm and steady enough to be able to eat anything.

"**B**E DARK SOON, thank God," Beard said. "We can relax an' stand easy soon as that ol' sun goes down."

"How's that?" Joseph asked. He was still crouching well below any line of sight from outside the enclosure, still terrified, but his voice held a measure of hope now at Beard's suggestion the danger was lessening.

"Injuns don't fight at night," Beard declared.

"You sure about that?"

"Ever'body knows that Injuns won't fight at night. Somethin' about the spirits not findin' their way to the Happy Huntin' Ground if they're kilt when it's dark."

Berrenton broke off a low-voiced conversation he was having with one of the Swiss and came over to join his troopers. "Are you serious about that, Beard? How do you know?"

"Oh, hell, Corp'r'l, that's something ever'body knows."

"I don't know it."

"Well, I do."

Berrenton grunted and went back to his conversation in halting German.

Hanson said nothing.

But he damn sure hoped the corporal did not intend to

act on Beard's so-called common knowledge and allow the men to relax their vigilance.

Modern armies did not fight at night either, at least not in the sense of conducting battles with lines drawn and banners waving. But patrols rode on their spying missions through the darkness, and skirmishers lay in wait for the unwary. Nighttime was even worse for fighting than the day. A man could not see his enemy so easily then, and he was quickly blinded by the brilliant light of his own muzzle flash. But at least he could see his enemy's muzzle discharges. How it would be to fight an enemy armed with bows that gave out no telltale flame when fired? Hanson did not like that thought.

Berrenton finished speaking with the Swiss and came over to his own men. "We're going to divide the watch tonight," he announced. "We'll take the first half of the night and let our friends there get some sleep. I gather they're pretty well worn out from all of them trying to stay awake ever since they holed up here, so we'll let them sleep, then wake them about midnight. They'll shake us out before dawn."

The corporal looked at Beard and added, "That's because everybody also knows that Indians like best to attack at dawn. Isn't that right, Trooper?"

Beard said nothing.

"Hanson, I want you to take post over there on the left. Then you, Ragen. Thames. Beard. Joseph over there. And I'll be on the far right next to Joseph. Everybody clear on that?"

No one said anything.

"Fine. Now finish eating or whatever you need to do. And mind, there'll be no smoking tonight. No noise. They know we're in here, but we don't have to make things any easier for them." He gave them a thin smile. "Just in case these particular Injuns don't know they aren't s'posed to fight in the dark."

The corporal nodded to his handful of troopers, then pointed at Joseph. "You, Private. Come with me. You and me are gonna see to the horses."

Berrenton took Joseph to the back of the fissure, beyond the horses to where the dead were laid out, their own Michael Kelly among them. The two stood there for some minutes in quiet conversation—Berrenton speaking and Joseph meekly listening—before they approached the horses.

Hanson nodded slightly to himself and leaned against a boulder at his assigned guard post with his carbine held loosely at the ready. The corporal was doing all right. For a damnyankee.

✛ 19 ✛

GOD, THE NIGHT watches were scary. Hanson's mouth was dry and his hands wet and his eyes burned from the effort of staring at gray and black nothing, trying to see shape or movement where none existed . . . or where anything that did move could prove deadly.

He licked his lips and swallowed back some of the bitter spit. It hit his stomach and turned that bitter, too. He felt like puking but knew better than to take his eyes away from the front where the Indians were.

A ways off, half a mile or so, he could see firelight reflected off one of the tall, straggly, thorn-covered things—cactus, tree, brush . . . he didn't know what the things were—that grew man high and at night, with light from the flames playing on them, took on the appearance of spectral beings.

At least in this dry and terrible country there were no clouds scudding overhead to make the night imaginings all the worse.

He could remember night watches back East when there was cloud casting moving shadows across a moonlit landscape. That was even worse than this. There'd been times when he would have sworn an oath that the haunts and the hobgoblins were out there. And every one of them after his blood and his soul.

That was worse. This was quite bad enough.

He heard one of the boys to his right cough and a moment later heard Berrenton's voice calm and soothing in the night, admonishing whichever trooper made the sound and at the same time encouraging their vigilance.

Probably there would be no stealthy attack tonight. Probably. Which did not mean that it couldn't happen or that they should relax the watch. Half on, half off. Troopers and Swiss. That was the sensible course.

Hanson pondered while he stared out into the blackness.

Did they have enough ammunition for this siege? Regulation issue was supposed to be sixty of the paper-tail cartridges for each man's carbine and eighteen for the revolvers. Except supplies hadn't yet caught up with need at Camp Lune, and they'd ridden off on patrol with only forty rounds for the carbines.

So far they'd fired . . . He tried to work it out. Couldn't. Maybe tomorrow he could slip a suggestion to the corporal that they count their cartridges and use them sparingly.

He just wished they had more ammunition for the revolvers. In this fight, the shorter accurate range of a revolver was more than compensated by the repeat-fire capability of the short guns. The sights on the issue Colts were set for an effective range of one hundred yards, and the guns were pretty accurate out to that distance if a man took his time aiming and kept a careful hold.

Perhaps they could break down some of the carbine cartridges and use the powder from those to charge the revolvers instead. If, that is, the corporal as patrol leader was issued a mold for casting balls for the .44 caliber revolvers. Carbine bullets wouldn't fit, but each one should surely provide enough lead to make two .44 balls. And the powder charges would be more than enough to divide into two revolver charges. Wrong size powder of course, but that shouldn't matter. If the corporal had a mold. If they had enough percussion caps for the revolvers, which took a cap smaller than the one that fit onto the Sharps nipples.

Tomorrow. He would ask Berrenton tomorrow. He—

The night was split apart by a flash of fire from the middle of the line of defense as someone's carbine roared, the sound unnaturally loud in what until that moment had been silence.

That first shot was followed instantly by two more.

Hanson had no target so did not fire. He squeezed his eyes tight shut for half a second, then opened them extra wide in an attempt to restore his night vision and find the attackers.

The Swiss came running from the back of the declivity where they'd been sleeping behind the horses, close to the bodies of the dead defenders.

There was a babble of German and one more gunshot.

Hanson still could find no target.

"Cease fire!" Berrenton bellowed. "Cease fire, goddammit. Joseph, you dumb sonuvabitch, what d'you think you're shooting at? There's no Injuns out there, you idiot."

No one else said anything, and after a few moments, the excitement waned and the disgruntled Swiss went back to their beds.

Joseph obviously fired at shadows.

Except there were no shadows moving. No clouds or breeze to cause any motion.

And within half a minute after the Swiss left, one then another and a third arrow came fluttering over the wall to land with short, ugly thumps into the ground.

The red bastards were out there. Somewhere. Hanson had no idea where.

So much, however, for Beard's theory that Indians never fight at night.

Hanson shuddered. And went back to his silent vigil.

✢ 20 ✢

THERE WAS NO attack in the night, nor did the anticipated dawn assault materialize. The Indians seemed quite content to keep the whites bottled up where they were. For now.

And why not? Why risk casualties when the enemy was thoroughly pinned in place waiting to be worn away by the slow attrition of arrows fired from a distance? A direct and serious attack would only expose the Indians to aimed fire from superior weapons.

The Indians, Hanson reminded himself, were savages. That did not necessarily mean they were stupid, too. It was a distinction he'd never given thought to before. Never needed to either, of course.

"All right, let's build up the fire, boys. Time for some breakfast," Berrenton called out in what sounded like a perfectly cheerful voice.

But then a soldier's mood is always elevated to find that he has survived another night. Daylight often breeds optimism.

"Beard, go bring some wood. Enough for one fire, not too big."

The trooper leaned his carbine against a rock, stood fully upright to take a look toward the flat scrubland where the Indians were hiding, and headed toward the makeshift mortuary at the back. Most of the available brush had been piled on top of the bodies to discourage birds from feasting on the corpses. As the brush was removed in order to make fires, they would soon have to start replacing it with soil.

"Corp'r'l." Beard sounded distressed.

Hanson turned to look. He supposed all of them did.

"Corp'r'l, it's your horse. Looka here."

"Aw . . . shit!" Berrenton's response was heartfelt and sorrowful. His mount, an ordinary remount animal that was nothing special to anyone but Jesse Berrenton, was down at its nigh hindquarter. The feathered stub of an arrow protruded from the ham. The horse must have been struck at some time during the night, and none of them had known.

Berrenton tried to get the animal to stand upright, but that back quarter simply could not support weight any longer. It was too much for the horse even to stand three legged, despite Berrenton's tugging and encouraging and cursing.

Hanson doubted that a crude arrow could break a horse's leg bone, but it was entirely possible that the missile had severed a critical nerve or something on that order. For whatever reason, the horse simply was not able to stand any longer.

Berrenton cast murderous looks off toward the Indians, but of course there was no way for him to retaliate. In the end all he could do was to unbutton his holster flap and take his revolver out.

"Wait, Corporal." Hanson set his carbine down, too, and hurried across the intervening yards.

"What d'you want, Hanson? He's suffering, dammit. I got to put him down."

"I know that, Corporal, and I'm sorry. Truly I am. But . . . let me take care of it, will you?"

"Why, Hanson?"

"Please, Corporal. You don't want to know why. Just let me do it. Then you'll understand."

"All right. All right." The corporal appeared relieved to have the distasteful burden taken off him. He took a moment to rub the horse's poll and to lightly scratch the sensitive hollow underneath the jaw, then steeled himself and returned to the firing line with the others.

Hanson, too, turned toward the front but only as far as the handcarts that belonged to the Swiss. He beckoned the nearest of the civilians, and that one brought their spokesman along in response.

Having no words in a common language Hanson mimed what he wanted. It took a minute for the Swiss to comprehend. Then the leader nodded vigorously and produced a tin box that he handed to Hanson.

"Thompson Farms Essence of Vegetable. The perfect food product. Desiccated with the most modern methods. Perfect for the preparation of soups or stews. May be powdered and used as a base for gravies or soups. Requires dry storage. Product of Thompson Farms, Warfordsburg, Penna."

Hanson borrowed a large pot from the Swiss's pile of baggage and returned to the corporal's horse.

He did not like doing it, but it had to be done. He unfolded his pocket knife and stropped it briefly on the side of his boot to make sure it would be as sharp as he could get it, then used the knife to open the large artery that runs on the underside of a horse's neck.

Blood spewed out in a strong flow. Hanson collected a half gallon or so in the pot, then regretfully allowed the rest to pump uselessly onto the ground as the horse weakened and slowly went to the ground.

Hanson looked into the huge, uncomplaining eyes and whispered, "Sorry, boy," not wanting the others to overhear.

He cleared his throat, impatient with himself, and poured the contents of the soup can into the fresh blood. Mixed it through with a stick and carried it to the fire to cook into a blood porridge. The result would undoubtedly taste like hell. But it would be rich in nourishment.

"Nathan."

"Yeah?" Joseph responded.

"Come over here and tend to this stew, would you?"

Joseph glanced toward Berrenton as if fearful the corporal would object to him leaving the firing line. Joseph himself seemed more than willing to take himself those few paces farther out of harm's way. When Berrenton ignored the request, Joseph hurried to the fire.

"Keep stirring it around so it cooks even, will you, Nathan?"

"You bet." Joseph hunkered low to the ground beside the fire, and Hanson returned to the corporal's horse, which by then was mercifully dead.

With a sigh he again took out his pocket knife and started the task of turning a large carcass into steaks for grilling over coals and thin strips for drying.

Not that they would likely be here long enough to need a supply of dried meat. But a man learns never to pass up an opportunity to acquire food or sleep or ammunition. Any of those can be crucial to his own survival.

HANSON LOOKED UP from his labor to find one of the Swiss standing over him with a long and rather wicked looking knife in his hand. Fortunately, the man was smiling. He transferred the knife to his left hand and extended his right. "Gerd," he said, presumably by way of introduction. Hanson shook his hand and returned the courtesy. The Swiss grinned and bobbed his head, then bent to the haunch Hanson had already skinned.

Gerd seemed to know what he was doing. Not only did he transform the carcass into steaks and strips, he did it with the quick efficiency of long practice. He babbled away in German while he worked, and Hanson assumed Gerd was explaining the finer points of proper butchering.

Not wanting to get in Gerd's way, Hanson used his own short pocket knife to resume the work of skinning. That seemed acceptable, but when he tried to cut some of the exposed meat into strips, Gerd touched Hanson's wrist and shook his head. "Nein, Hantzon, nein."

Hanson finished skinning everything he could reach, cut off a generous flap of hide, and piled the entrails onto that so he could drag the rather smelly mess as far to the rear as he could get it. He started trying to kick gravel over top of it and was stopped again by one of the Swiss, this time a burly man who introduced himself as Karl. He was carrying a small shovel, a rather compact and cunning little thing with a spade head not much bigger than a man's hand and a handle that folded to make it even smaller for packing. Rather than offering the shovel to Hanson, Karl leaned down and undertook the labor himself. Hanson admired that. These Swiss were willing to pitch in with their share of the hard work.

By the time Hanson and the two Swiss returned to the front of their little fortress, the stew had finished cooking. Someone, Joseph probably, had removed it from the fire and set the pot aside.

No one, however, was eating the dark and lumpy but rather pleasantly aromatic blood pudding.

Hanson said nothing to them. He went to his own small roll of personal possessions and fetched his mess plate and a spoon. He helped himself to a generous portion of the pudding and stepped back, then tried a bite. The mixture tasted considerably better than he'd expected. In fact, it was quite good. Hanson grinned and smacked his lips and winked at Nathan Joseph, who was watching him with horrified fascination.

"Yummy," Hanson mumbled around another mouthful.

After a few minutes, Heuer joined him and took some of the blood pudding. He said something to the other Swiss, then to Hanson added, "Goot. Very goot."

The other Swiss came and spooned out portions of the stew. After a few minutes more, Thames and Ragen tried some. Berrenton did not, no surprise there as it had been his horse, nor did Nathan Joseph.

They let the fire die out but laid some steaks on the coals. Hanson and Gerd spent the remainder of the morning draping strips of meat onto almost every immobile surface in reach.

✠ 22 ✠

"THEY'RE UP TO something," Berrenton called, bringing the squad members' attention to the front again. The corporal said something else in German, and the Swiss, too, got up from a card game and hurried to the wall just like the troopers were doing.

Hanson took his assigned spot, anchoring the far left end of the thin line. To his right he could hear the clatter of hammers being cocked and throats being cleared. Someone muttered a curse in German. Hanson did not need to know the words in order to understand that tone of voice.

Far to the front, too far to have any reasonable chance with aimed fire, he could see a cloud of dust approaching.

"It's the lieutenant an' the rest of the troop." Hanson thought the voice was Thames's.

"No, it ain't," Berrenton said calmly. "It's too soon to be our boys."

"You think the Injuns is pulling out?"

"Nope. Dust is coming this way. Could be more Indians. It damn sure don't mean less."

"I still think it's our boys. They're moving fast, that's all."

"Think whatever you please, but keep that carbine ready, you hear me, Private?"

"Yes, Corporal. I hear you."

Hanson remained at his post, but he allowed himself to relax just the same. If the Indians were receiving reinforcements, that would surely be bad news in the long run, but for right now it probably meant that the bunch who had the squad bottled up here would be distracted from the business of fighting at least for the time being. They would want to welcome the newcomers and show off their position.

Actually, if the Swiss only had horses, this might not be a bad time to try to break out. Before the new crowd arrived and while most of the original bunch were pulled back away from the siege in order to say hello to these others.

The squad was short on mounts what with one missing out there with the Indians, one dead in here and drying in the sun, and one other injured. But the men could double up long enough for a dash while the savages were distracted. Then . . .

He scowled. Then! Then nothing. Even if they tried—and that was ignoring the problem of the ground-pounding Swiss—there was no damn place to run to. The Indians would only give pursuit, and with the troopers' horses having to carry double, that would be short-lived indeed . . . as would be the men themselves.

Escape was pure fantasy, Hanson conceded. Until the troop arrived to break the siege, the best they could hope for was to hold the savages at bay.

Hold out. Hold on. Be ready to offer supporting fire when the troop came charging in.

That was all they could hope for.

Hanson turned and looked toward the rear where the horses stood hipshot and listless. They hadn't had proper food or water since they got here, and soon the effects of that abuse would begin to show.

For right now, though, for this afternoon and probably never again afterward, Hanson's horse might well be strong enough and swift enough to make a break for freedom and safety.

Carrying one man only.

The Indians out front there would be slow to respond. Their horses were not near. The savages would have to run on foot for a quarter mile or more just to reach their ponies. And their attention would be on the arrival of these other Indians anyway.

One man . . . they might not even bother to disrupt the siege in order to chase one man. They might not want to take the cork out of the bottle by breaking away to chase a lone escapee.

One man just might be able to get away. By himself.

Hanson clenched his jaw. Just how damned much did he owe these Yankee soldiers anyway? He'd accepted their parole. He'd put on their uniform and taken their orders.

And now . . .

"Shit!" he snarled, not realizing he was saying it aloud until he heard the sound himself.

"Something wrong, Hanson?" Ragen asked.

"Aside from the fact that it looks like another thirty or forty Indians are coming to join this first crowd? Aside from the fact that I got heat galls in my armpits and my whiskers itch like hell and that I'd like to have a beer one more time before I die?" He shook his head. "No, Albert, I expect everything's just fine and dandy, thank you."

Ragen chuckled and spat a stream of tobacco juice over the wall.

Hanson grimaced. He'd accepted their parole. He was a part of the squad.

And if a man's word has no meaning, then nothing else does either.

He watched the new band of Indians come closer.

✠ 23 ✠

"**W**HAT'RE THE SONS o' bitches doing, having a party?"

"Sounds like it."

The two bands of Indians were shrieking and shouting and deliberately showing themselves dancing in a circle around a fire to the accompaniment of some drums. The whole thing was being carried out a good quarter mile away, out of rifle shot from the forted-up whites.

"If we had one of those long-barrel Sharps with glass sights, we could get us one of the bastards. Teach them to jump around like that."

"Yeah, and if we had a brass band and some cannon we could have us a helluva celebration, too."

Hanson said nothing. He only watched. And frowned. He'd heard about those heavy Sharps rifles with the magnifying-glass sights on them. Never saw one close up, but he'd seen the work they could do. He'd lost two close friends to one of those long-shooting specialists. Sharp-shooters, they were being called nowadays. Had their own special outfit run by a colonel named Berdan. Hanson knew. He'd asked about the damnyankee sons of bitches first thing after they took him and put him in their prison.

But Thames was right. If they had even one of those rifles now . . .

He sighed. They didn't. That was the fact of the matter. All they had were their revolvers and carbines, neither of them any good at long distances, and not a whole hell of a lot of ammunition for them either.

Hanson absently fiddled in the pouch that held the paper cartridges for his Colt revolver. He had thirteen rounds left. He already knew that. He kept counting them over and over again anyway. It was something to keep him occupied while he waited for the Indians to come.

Berrenton left his position on the far right side and motioned for Hanson to join him at the back of the enclosure.

"Yes, Corporal?"

"You've never fought Indians, Hanson?"

He couldn't help it. "No, Corporal. Just Yankees."

Berrenton chose to ignore that. "D'you have any thoughts about what we can expect now that they have reinforcements out there?"

"It'd only be guesses."

"That's all right. You know more about combat than the rest of us. Tell me what you would guess."

"All right. I think the first bunch will want to show their pals how tight they have us pinned in here. I think the whole crowd will make a run at us. But I don't think they'll be real serious about carrying a charge to the wall, Corporal. You can see how they're dancing and howling out there. They're having themselves a good time now. Aren't worried about us at all. I think they figure they can wear us down and take as long as need be to do it. So if I was in command of the squad and could speak a little German, I guess what I'd tell everybody is they should hold their fire when the Indians come. Not completely, or they'll get bold and finish things here and now. But I think you should tell everybody to fire once, reload and not fire again unless they think they have to. Nobody should spend more than two rounds when the Indians come. Which reminds me. I wanted to mention a couple things to you anyway, since we got so little ammunition with us."

Hanson made his suggestion about converting carbine cartridges for double use in the revolvers, but Berrenton shook his head about that idea. "We don't have a bullet mold to recast the lead. Don't have very many extra caps in the Colt size either, I'm afraid. Otherwise I'd say it was a good idea, and if we were back at Camp Lune, we could do it." He smiled. "I'm afraid it will be a couple days yet before we see Lune again."

"Permission to speak, Corporal?"

"Yes, of course."

"I want you to know, Corporal. I've served under worse leadership than you."

Berrenton blinked. "I . . . thank you, Hanson. Coming from you, that means a lot to me."

"Yes, well . . ."

"You can go on back to your post. I'll warn the others what to expect and tell them to conserve their ammunition as best they can. I'll tell the Swiss, too, of course, but they're free to do whatever they please."

"That guy with the shotgun can fire pebbles or anything that comes to hand, so if they have a decent supply of powder and caps, he probably ought to show as much smoke as he can get out of the thing."

"All right. Yes."

Hanson went back to his place, and Berrenton walked the length of the wall, speaking with each man in turn until the corporal was back at his post, too.

The Swiss already had Michael Kelly's carbine and revolver, so they were better armed than when the squad arrived. The whites were still undergunned for what might be needed here.

"Jesus, I hope Vickers gets back with the troop soon," Joseph said to no one in particular. "I sure hope they come soon."

Out on the desert floor, the Indians continued to dance and taunt.

✝ 24 ✝

"U H-OH!" HANSON MUTTERED.

"I see them," Berrenton responded. "Let's stay awake now, boys. It looks like they'll be coming now."

The Indians left off their dancing and jumped onto their ponies. The men could get a good look at their foe once they were on horseback and clearly visible above the brush and rolling contours of the ground. It was a daunting sight. There were scores of them out there, a force that was probably between fifty and sixty strong.

"Remember what I told you, boys. Hold your fire. Hold your fire."

One of the Swiss said something, too. Judging from his tone of voice, Hanson guessed the German words carried much the same message as Berrenton's English had.

"Uh-huh."

Out in front, the swarm of savages began to move, and the whooping and shouting became all the louder. Hanson cocked his carbine, then laid it down on the stone breastworks so he would not be so tempted to aim and fire. This was but a probe instead of an attack. Or so he hoped and believed. If it was not, if this was a concerted and serious assault, well, they would have to shoot hot and heavy to keep that many from overwhelming them.

Something occurred to him, and Hanson raised his voice as the squadron of nearly naked savages surged in a hard run straight at their little fortress. He had to shout in order to be heard above the thunder of so many hoofs. "Don't shoot the horses, men. We don't want to give them anything to hide behind. Make damn sure you don't bring down any horses."

The Indians came on, yipping and howling, sweeping from the left front across to the right and out again, some of them coming so close Hanson could have thrown rocks at them.

The charge was the damnedest display of horsemanship Hanson ever saw. As they wheeled to cross the front of the defensive work, the Indians somehow were able to drop completely out of sight, clinging like ticks on the far side of their mounts.

Not shoot any horses? There were no targets in sight other than horses. The riders popped upright again once they were past the white men's guns and headed back toward their own lines once more.

Several of the boastful sons of bitches dropped their breechclouts and showed their naked asses toward the enemy as they galloped safely away.

The squad held their discipline as Berrenton encouraged them in a deep-throated damnyankee growl, but the Swiss who had been given Kelly's carbine dropped one of the Indian ponies. His shot struck the animal in the side of the head, and it flew into a sprawling somersault, throwing its rider high into the air. The Swiss with the shotgun must have been a fowler experienced with shooting birds on the wing, because his gun roared and slapped a pattern of heavy shot into the Indian before the man's body ever hit the ground. The Indian was already dead when he landed, striking with that limp finality that cannot be faked or at least not by anyone Hanson ever heard of.

"Damn fine shooting," he called out.

Beard loosed a round in the general direction of the Indians, the last of whom had made their approach and were headed away again.

"They're coming again," Hanson shouted.

"Hold fire, boys," Berrenton ordered. He said something in German, and Heuer called out instruction to his people, too.

There were fewer Indians in this second wave, and they came even nearer to the wall.

Eighteen or twenty of them rushed in, wheeled left, and raced across the front as before.

Again the whites were treated to the sight of naked copper asses.

"Jesus!" Ragen blurted as the Indians departed. "Look." He was pointing toward the ground in front of the wall.

The body of the Indian they'd killed the day before was gone. So was that of the one the shotgunner nailed. The second wave of horsemen somehow grabbed up both while traveling at a dead run.

"Well I'll be a son of a bitch."

Hanson shuddered, happy he had the protection of solid rock in front of him, because these Indians would be one formidable foe in a fight from horseback.

"Did we take any casualties?" Berrenton called. "Is anyone hurt?"

"Y'know, Corp'r'l, I don't remember any of the bastards shooting at us. Not one arrer."

Hanson didn't either, now that he thought about it. The whole thing was an exercise in bravado and intimidation. And judging by the darkly wet crotch and leg of Nathan Joseph's britches, the Indians certainly accomplished that much.

Hanson carefully let the hammer of his Sharps down to half cock. He was shivering. And it damn sure was not cold.

✢ 25 ✢

THE MEN SAT in small groups, both the troopers and the Swiss, with the conversation dominated by the subject of those Indians and their abilities on horseback. But then no wonder. Hanson never saw anyone ride like that before either, and he thought he knew a little about campaigning on horseback.

"Corporal?"

"Yes?"

"Are those guys talking about the same things we are?" Hanson used the term *we* even though he was not included in any of the groupings of soldiers. The blueleg boys did not consider him one of them. That was fair enough. He did not really think of himself as one of them either.

"Yeah, they are." Berrenton puffed on his pipe for a moment, then said, "Beard, I want you to collect a little water from each man. We're gonna brew us up a pot of coffee. Coffee will go good about now, I think."

"You think we oughta use the water thataway, Corporal?" Joseph asked. His trousers were nearly dry now, and he seemed to be feeling better knowing he was still alive.

"We need something to drink," Berrenton said, "and it might as well be coffee." The corporal smiled. "Besides, the troop should be getting here this afternoon or some time tonight. Once we're relieved, we can get all the water we want."

Hanson had no idea just exactly where Berrenton thought they were going to find all that water except in the canteens of the men in the relief column, but he said nothing. Berrenton was right that they needed to drink something to keep their strength up and was right as well that it might as well be in the form of coffee. There is something about the smell of boiling coffee that soothes much more than a man's belly. It does much for his peace of mind, too.

Hanson contributed his share into the coffee pan, then picked up the empty pot the blood pudding had been in. The pot not only had been emptied, it was scraped almost clean. Hanson took it over to the side of the fortress floor to a spot where he'd seen some gravel so fine it was almost sand. He knelt there and used a handful of the gritty material to scrub and polish the metal, then used the tail of his shirt to wipe it out.

The pot belonged to the Swiss, so he took it back to the camp they'd made for themselves before the troopers arrived. He lifted a square of canvas in the handcart and returned the article where he found it.

Except, he saw now, this was not the same cart. And the things that lay beneath that bit of canvas were not cooking implements.

"Jesus God!" Beard blurted from beside the fire where he was watching over the coffee. "Is that what I think it is?"

Hanson, too, gasped.

Before he had time to respond, he sensed a shape coming at him from the side and had time enough, if barely, to brace himself before the big Swiss named Karl charged into him and bowled him off his feet.

The Swiss were shouting wildly in German, and the boys in the squad were screaming back at them, and somebody—Ragen, Hanson thought moments before he was able to scramble back onto his feet and throw himself into the fray beside the others—began throwing punches, and before any of them had time to think, there was a melee raising dust and tempers in roughly equal proportions.

"At ease! At ease, goddammit!" Berrenton roared above the sounds of the scrapping. "What the hell has gotten into you people? Thames, Ragen, get back on that wall and pay attention to what's going on out there. That is where the enemy is, damn you all. Now what is this about?"

Heuer was sputtering at him in German, and Beard was babbling at him in English, and Berrenton obviously could not make a lick of sense out of either of them.

"Dammit, slow down here. Beard, you shut up." He listened to Heuer for a couple minutes, then turned back to Hanson. "He says he saw you looking in their personal possessions."

"I was putting the stewpot away, Corporal. It's still there. Look for yourself."

"That ain't all that's there, Corp'r'l. That ain't all."

"Whatever are you jabbering about now, Beard?"

"Gold, Corp'r'l. There's bags o' gold in that cart. Look for ye'self if you don't believe me an' Johnny Reb here."

Heuer said something, and the Swiss congealed into a tight knot surrounding the handcart in question.

Gold!

The single word sent a lightning-bolt charge of electricity through the troopers of the squad.

26

THE DAMNED SQUAREHEADS had their guns in hand and were bristling like a bunch of mother bears looking out for their cubs.

The guy with the shotgun would be the most dangerous, Hanson figured, and if it came to shooting, he was the one Hanson figured to take down first. If he could. A shotgun is formidable, and this man was not afraid to kill. He'd already demonstrated that during the Indian charge.

But then Hanson had made his own demonstrations. And to men whose opinion he valued above that of any son of a bitch here. If it came down to it, they would just have to see what Hanson's revolver could do against the Swiss's scattergun.

Heuer was yammering something in German, and Berrenton was standing between the two sides, and the troopers looked as ready to explode as the Swiss did. One accidental slip of a trigger finger would be about all it would take to launch a bloodbath, and if that happened, the only ones who could possibly benefit would be the Indians.

Hanson peered out over the wall, hesitated for only a moment, and then shouted, "Injuns! Look out!"

He ran to the wall and grabbed up his carbine, thumbing the hammer back and snapping a shot into the empty grass beyond the dead horse lying out there.

The reaction of the troopers and of the civilians was what he'd hoped. They set aside their worries for the moment and ran to form a common defense.

Thames and two of the Swiss fired at nothing, too, their imaginations supplying targets that the Indians did not. Hanson did not consider those cartridges wasted though.

He sidled over to Berrenton and stood there, carbine in one hand and revolver in the other, ready in case the corporal needed any help.

Berrenton, fortunately, was up to the task. The corporal might not have much combat experience, but this was a matter of handling men, and he could handle that just fine.

"Cease fire, goddammit, cease fire. They're gone to ground again." He glanced at Hanson, obviously aware of what the galvanized trooper had done. And why. When he turned again to his troopers, his voice held the hard edge of unquestionable authority. "Maybe those bags in that cart there hold gold. Maybe they don't. Herr Heuer says they don't. Point is, whether they do or not, it ain't *your* gold any more than it's mine, and you aren't thieves. You're cavalry troopers in the United States Army, and you're here to protect these civilians . . . protect them *and* whatever they own . . . from those redbelly savages out there. This afternoon, maybe tonight, the lieutenant will get here with the troop and relieve us from this siege. When that happens, I want cause to be proud of every one of you. You hear what I'm saying here? Do you take my meaning? God help you if you don't, because I won't hesitate if I have to write you up on charges, and I can tell you plain that no one is gonna take those bags of . . . whatever . . . from these civilians without a fight. They won't be taken except over the dead bodies of the men who worked for them. That would mean I'd personally be filing murder charges against any man that raises a hand against these civilians. Are you hearing me? The army hangs soldiers that murder civilians. Except I wouldn't let it get that far. I'd shoot you down my own damn self before I'd let it come to that. Now, I suggest you forget about things that don't belong to you and pay attention to those Indians out there. They *are* a soldier's business."

Berrenton glared at his troopers until one by one they rather sheepishly turned their attention back out onto the sere, sun-baked landscape before them. Then the corporal gave his attention to the Swiss, speaking with Heuer and the others in slow and careful German.

It took some persuading, but eventually the Swiss relaxed. Their expressions lost the dark, hooded pugnaciousness, and they let the muzzles of their weapons down. A little longer, and most of them returned to their places along the wall, all except Heuer, who seemed to have been appointed to sit on the rim of the handcart that held the gold.

Hanson went back to his place, too. He laid his carbine back where it had been and removed his campaign hat to let a little air reach his scalp. The heat galls in his armpits and groin were throbbing again, and he would have mortgaged his soul for a bath and a shave.

27

IF IT WEREN'T for the damned Indians, this wouldn't be such a bad campaign. After all, soldiers are generally at their happiest when their bellies are full and they certainly had plenty of food in the camp now. And not only was there a gracious plenty to eat, Berrenton's horse even tasted pretty good.

They'd had steak for the noon meal and now again in the evening, the dark red meat speared on a cleaning rod and grilled over live flame. Berrenton, Hanson noticed, had succumbed to the tempting smell of cooked meat and joined them now. Apparently he liked steak better than he'd liked the horse.

As dusk turned into dark, the Indians, too, had a fire going. Not the half dozen or so small fires that they'd built the night before but one really big one. The flames rose a good five or six feet high.

"Man, they must've drug wood in from ten miles around to get that big a fire," Ragen observed around a chew of tobacco.

"I say they couldn't of found that much inside twenty miles," Thames put in. "They prob'ly imported it."

"Where the hell from?"

"I dunno. Pennsylvania maybe. They got lots of trees in Pennsylvania."

"You're full of shit, Chris."

"Sure I am. So what?"

Ragen laughed. "You think when we get out of here you and me could apply for the firewood supply contract for those Injuns? Buy cheap, sell dear. That's what my old daddy used to say."

"Businessman, is he?"

"Yes, and a good one, too. He's started a new business 'most every year since I can remember. Starts up in springtime. Goes bankrupt before winter. Happens every year." Ragen spat over the wall and scratched his crotch. He probably had heat galls, too, Hanson suspected.

"They've started dancing again," Hanson observed aloud.

Out in front a quarter mile, the Indians had begun yelping and dancing, circling the fire around and around.

"I bet I could put a bullit raht in there," Beard said.

"Don't," Berrenton told him from the far end of the wall. "Even if you could hit something, it would only stir them up. We're better off to let them alone until the relief column gets here. That big fire will help guide the lieutenant in, and we'll have them caught between us and the troop, be able to get some of our own back for their damned deviltry."

The dancing continued, but the shouting died down.

After a few minutes of silence the evening quiet was pierced by a chilling shriek.

"What the hell was that?" Thames asked. The Swiss were murmuring among themselves, too.

The scream, loud and quavering, sounding like it was ripped out of the pits of Hell, was repeated. And again.

"What *is* going on out there?"

"I think somebody should walk out an' ask them. I appoint you for the job, Beard."

The voice rose again, louder this time. There was something in it that made Hanson shudder.

"Some kind of religious rite maybe?" he mused aloud.

The next scream was weaker. And another after that weaker still.

"Jesus," Beard said. Joseph crossed himself and hunkered down against the base of a boulder with his hands pressed over his ears.

Hanson looked at the bit of steak he still held. For some reason, his appetite was gone. He tossed the seared meat out into the night where some bird or small creature would find it. His mouth was dry and his stomach unsettled.

There were several minutes of silence and then another scream.

"I overheard once a woman givin' birth. She screamed somethin' awful but not as bad as that. D'you think . . . ?"

"They ain't got no women out there giving birth," Ragen said.

"Could be they've chose one of them for an, I don't know, an offering maybe? Like, a sacrifice?"

"Do Injuns have religion?"

"Damn if I know."

"They have religion," Hanson said. "I read something about that once."

"D' they make sacrifices?"

"The old-time Aztecs did. They're the ones I read about. They killed people, babies even, cut their chests open and ripped their hearts out while the victim was still alive."

"Jesus God."

"But this bunch can't be Aztecs. There aren't any of them left, the book said."

"You think these bastards ever read that book o' yours, Hanson?"

Another scream tore the fabric of the night, and again

Hanson shuddered. Whatever ceremony those Indians were up to, he did not like it.

The scream came again, weaker this time.

The men stood at their posts, riveted, wide awake and attentive, braced for the next shriek. But none came. After half an hour it became apparent that the Indians were allowing their bonfire to die down.

"All right, boys. Let's get some sleep. The Swiss are going to take the first watch tonight since we did it last night. Go on now. But sleep with your weapons just in case something happens."

"Yes, Corp'r'l."

"Yo."

Hanson paused to send another worried look out toward what was left of the ceremonial fire. Then he made his way to the spot he'd hollowed out in the gravel to serve as a bed.

Hot as the days were here, the nights were cold. He shivered and wrapped his blanket close around him.

28

HE HEARD A gasp from his right, and a moment later he saw why.

"Lookit that son of a bitch," someone whispered.

It was true there was someone out there. Standing stock still and probably believing that he wouldn't be seen as long as he did not move. Observing, Hanson guessed. Planning deviltry for tomorrow.

He was close. Not more than fifty or sixty yards away.

There were some high clouds drifting on the wind, and the desert had been silent and empty. Then a cloud cut off the thin, watery light of the half moon. Moments later, when the cloud passed, the dark, motionless figure was there. A man shape, plain as plain could be.

But of course anyone standing out there and looking toward the mesa where the whites were forted up would find it darker than did the men inside the fortress looking out onto the desert. Here was the black and gray of stone. There the pale tans and yellows of grass and soil. Obviously the Indian believed himself to be unobserved.

But he was a cheeky SOB to stand there like that. And brave. Hanson wondered if he'd been one who showed his butt during that crazy charge.

Over the sound of loud snoring from one of the Swiss,

he could hear Berrenton moving along the thin line of
troopers at the wall during this predawn watch. When the
corporal reached Hanson, he leaned close to Hanson's ear
and whispered, "I want you to hold your fire. In a minute
I'm going to give the command and most of us will shoot.
We're going to give that Injun a hot breakfast. But I want
you and Joseph to stay loaded and ready in case there's
others thinking to come in once our guns are empty."

Hanson nodded and drew his revolver. If there was a
charge, he wanted its greater firepower rather than the
heavier impact of the Sharps bullet.

Berrenton went back the way he'd come. Hanson
closed one eye to preserve his night vision. There was a
minute or so of silence. Then, "Now!"

The night erupted into sheets of yellow flame as three
carbines roared.

The Swiss came bellowing and stumbling off their
beds, and two of them also fired, although Hanson
doubted they had any idea what they were shooting at.
He hadn't been prepared for that, hadn't kept his eye
closed, and so for several unnerving moments had no
night vision whatsoever.

He blinked and pressed the heels of his hands tight
against his eyes, thumping himself rather hard with the
grips of the Colt when he did so but almost frantic to
regain the ability to see at least a little.

He needn't have bothered.

When he could see again, he was able to see that the
man-shape was still there, unmoving and unmoved.

"We couldn't 've missed, Corp'r'l."

"You didn't miss, Beard. Not everybody surely." He
sounded disgusted. "The red bastards are having their fun
with us." He turned and repeated that in German for the
benefit of the Swiss, and the civilians went grumbling
back to bed.

"Teasing us," Hanson said, "or maybe being clever.

Now that we know it isn't somebody standing there, one of them could sneak up and stand behind that dummy to look us over, knowing we won't shoot again. Get himself a real good, long look before daybreak."

Beard raised his carbine and fired at the dark shape again.

The Swiss jumped up for a second time, but Berrenton calmed them, then told Beard, "Don't do that again, Private. Let these men get some sleep."

Hanson looked at the sky. It would be a good two hours or more before dawn. Call it an hour and a half before there was enough light to begin expecting whatever the Indians were up to. But any time after that . . .

"Stay awake now, boys. Don't shoot at the dummy again, but be alert. We know they're moving around, and they got something in mind, damn them. So keep your eyes open. Be ready."

Berrenton went back to his post on the far right, and the line gradually settled down into the weary ennui of late-night guard duty.

Hanson returned the Colt to its holster and leaned against the cold, gritty stone of the wall. Damn, but it was difficult to stay alert, even after the heart-pounding excitement a few minutes earlier.

What was it they said about soldiering? Months of numbing boredom relieved by occasional bursts of stark terror. That was about it, too.

He yawned and rubbed his eyes. He would have given up ten years of his life for a bath and a long, cool drink.

If, that is, he had ten years of living left to barter with.

29

"NO. DEAR GOD, no."

Hanson felt sick to his stomach. Thames began to cry and Ragen to curse. Beard looked like he wanted to do both.

A thin sliver of golden sun edged into view on the eastern horizon, and the desert began to take on shape and color.

And they were able to see the object the Indians placed in front of them during the small hours of the morning.

It was no brush and cloth dummy that was propped up on a tripod of short poles.

It was a human form. A naked, hideously mutilated human body.

A body, Hanson noted, that was viciously battered and stripped of part of its skin and yet had been—deliberately, he was sure—left with the features recognizable.

Vickers. The trooper who'd been sent as a courier to Camp Lune to alert the troop and bring back a relief column.

"He didn't . . . oh, God, I shot him. I shot Harry!"

"He was already dead, son. Don't think like that."

"It was Harry we heard screaming last night, wasn't it?"

"Probably. Yes, it probably was."

Ragen looked toward the sky. "Please, God. Damn their souls to the fire. Please."

"Likely he ran into the second bunch. No telling why they brought him back here with them. Maybe they got him to tell them what he was doing," Berrenton said. "The point is, boys, there'll be no troop coming to pull our fat out of this fire. It's up to us alone." He turned and spoke with Heuer and the other Swiss for a while.

The Swiss, Hanson saw, looked every bit as sickened by the sight of Vickers as the troopers.

The only mercy, such as it was, was that Vickers's body was far enough away that they could not see in complete and terrible detail the agonies he'd suffered before death allowed him to escape from his tormentors.

As it was, they could see more than enough. Joseph went to the back of the area where they'd dug a latrine. He fell to his knees and began throwing up. It surprised no one, Hanson was sure, that Private Joseph remained there at the back of the enclosure, puking and weeping and probably pissing himself.

This time he certainly had reason, however.

"Damn them," Hanson found himself saying along with the others. "Damn them, every one."

He found it incredible—in the true meaning of that word, literally beyond credibility—that any human being could do such vile and terrible things to another living creature. Any sort of live thing, far less another human.

But then, he considered, perhaps that right there explained it. Perhaps the red savages were not human. Not in any sense that he would recognize.

"We have to cut him down off of there," Ragen said.

"No!" Berrenton snapped. "They'd love for us to go out and try just that. They'll be out there waiting for us. Count on it."

"Then we should shoot the legs off the poles, Corporal.

They aren't very sturdy looking. One or two bullets ought to do it, and we wouldn't have to bust all of them. If we can break just one it . . . Harry . . . will fall down. We got to try it, Corporal."

"No, dammit. We don't have ammunition to waste."

"It wouldn't be no waste, Corporal. We just got to—"

"No!" Berrenton's voice was sharp almost to the point of hysteria, and that frightened Hanson far more than the sight of Trooper Vickers's tortured body. If Berrenton lost control of the squad, they had no chance at all.

Not that they likely had any chance anyway. But without discipline, the Indians' victory would be inescapable and probably very quick.

"Tonight," Hanson said. "We'll wait for night. Then I'll creep out there and cut him down."

"You can't—"

Hanson gave Ragen a grim smile. "Yeah, I can. You don't know how many times I've snuck into Yankee camps and stole coffee from you sons of bitches." Did other things, too, actually but there was no point in going into detail about any of that.

Heuer said something, and the corporal turned his attention to the civilians.

Hanson motioned for Beard to join him and went to cut some more steaks off Berrenton's horse before the meat became too spoiled for use. The smell of the carcass told him it was already on the ragged edge of rot. Both of them ignored Joseph, who was still on his knees blubbering and dripping snot.

"Reb," Beard said in a small voice as he knelt over the coals to restart the fire.

"Yeah, John?"

"Did you shoot him, too, Reb?"

"We all did, John. If it makes you feel any better, remember that a man can't aim worth a damn in the dark.

Likely your bullet missed hitting him." Hanson didn't believe that, but he hoped Beard would.

"Yeah. Maybe it did at that."

"How many steaks do we need here anyway?"

"Don't cut one for him," Beard said, inclining his head toward Joseph. "Little bastard don't deserve to eat with decent men."

"Aw, whoever heard of a decent damnyankee," Hanson said with a grin. "If I was to go by that, just me and those squareheads would eat."

Beard laughed just a little and seemed to take no offense.

Hanson did carve a steak for Joseph, though, despite Beard's objections. When the time came for him to choose between fighting and dying, Joseph would probably fight right along with the rest of them. He damn sure hoped so anyway.

✛ 30 ✛

THE INDIANS WAITED a good two hours or more past full daylight before they came. Wanted to let the whites fret and tremble for a while first, Hanson supposed.

There was no stealth about it this time. The assault was preceded by dancing and stomping and shouted insults as the red men worked themselves into a crazed and frantic state.

One warrior became overly worked up. He ran in close, whirled around, and dropped his breechclout in the now-familiar gesture of contempt.

Hanson laid his Sharps on top of the wall for a steady rest, aimed and squeezed with care, and shot the Indian squarely in the ass. "Up yours," he said aloud.

Beard laughed. "I think that's right where it went, too, Reb."

"Stand ready, boys, but don't fire until I give the word," Berrenton warned in a calm, steady voice. "We can't be wasting any ammunition. Remember. We got only ourselves to rely on. There won't be any relief column, so we got to make those bastards pay so heavy each time they come near that they'll give it up and leave us be."

The corporal said something, presumably the same

message, in German and got back an approving murmur from the Swiss.

Out in front, the Indians' whooping and taunting reached a crescendo, and the dam burst into a screaming frenzy.

With a mad cacophony of screeching, the massed Indians charged forward on foot.

Didn't want to risk their horses, Hanson thought. He felt slightly detached from the scene. Aloof and apart and quite calm. It was like that sometimes. It wasn't bravery. More a matter of simply not being there along with the others, at least not in his own mind and emotions.

He watched the Indians run. Chose a target from among those in the fore, and again took careful aim.

He saw his ball strike the red man just above his breastbone, roughly at the base of the throat. Before the Indian's body struck the earth in a facedown sliding fall, Hanson was reloading. Drop the finger lever. Push a cartridge into the chamber. Make sure the paper tail was extended into the loading chute. Lift the lever again, the sharp edge of the breachblock slicing off the tail to expose the powder charge within. Draw the hammer to half cock. Pluck a musket cap from the pouch and fit it onto the nipple. Thumb the hammer the rest of the way back to full cock. Present weapon. Aim. Squeeze. Don't jerk. Squeeze.

Another Indian went down.

But, Lord, they were closer now. Dozens of them. A hundred? No, that was an exaggeration. Scores of them though. Scores.

He lay the Sharps down and drew his Colt. Aimed. Fired.

Missed, dammit.

Aim again. Fire again. That was better. The ball struck that one in the belly. Good. That would take him out of the fight and occupy at least two of the others dragging him back to safety.

Aim. Fire.

The burnt gunpowder, so sweet a smell in small quantities, filled his nostrils until it reeked. He had the sharp taste of it on his tongue.

Sweat rolled stinging into his eye and he was not sure if he hit with his fourth pistol shot. No time to worry about that.

Damn, but they were close now.

He shot one in the face from a distance of less than ten yards.

Brought the Colt to half cock and spun the cylinder two clicks to expose the loaded but uncapped sixth nipple. Pressed one of the small revolver-size foil caps in place. Turned the cylinder again. Cocked. Aimed. Fired.

Damn it. The hammer dropped with no effect on a chamber already fired. He hadn't turned the cylinder far enough. Or turned it too far. Damn it anyway. He looked down to determine where the fresh cap glimmered brightly at the back of the cylinder. There. Good.

He cocked the revolver again. Snapped a shot into the chest of a man who was within two or three steps. The Indian kept coming and was trying to climb over the wall with a club in hand. Hanson grabbed up his empty Sharps and gave the red man a butt stroke hard enough to stun an ox. The front of the Indian's face caved in with a crunch, and he dropped out of sight on the other side of the wall.

Hanson reloaded the Sharps.

Aimed. Fired. But this time he was aiming at an Indian's back. The charge was broken. The Indians were running.

Hanson was panting, his ribs aching and his chest heaving as he gulped for breath. He felt like he'd just completed a hard sprint of his own.

"Jesus!" It was Ragen's voice, but Hanson agreed. Thoroughly.

He reloaded the Sharps first, then the Colt. There were damned few cartridges left for the Colt. Come to that, there weren't an awful lot left for the carbine either.

"Thank goodness," Hanson said.

"Is everybody all right? Johnny. Johnny? Get up, will you?"

Hanson looked. Beard wouldn't be getting up again. The front of his skull was crushed. One of the Indians had gotten close enough to club him. It was not a pretty way to die. Not that any way really is.

And two of the Swiss were down. One lay writhing in pain with an arrow in his belly. That one would die, Hanson knew. Another had been shot in the throat and lay now in a pool of his own blood.

The Indians had been repulsed, but Hanson could not claim that the defenders had scored any sort of victory over them. There were still plenty of Indians out there. Now there were fewer whites to stand against the next charge.

Hanson looked out onto the desert in an effort to see just how many Indians they'd killed.

There was not a body in sight. None. The Indians had already carried off their dead and their wounded.

Hanson even stood on tiptoes and risked peeking over the wall to the ground where he knew damned good and well he'd deposited a thoroughly dead Indian warrior not five minutes ago.

The gravel there was empty save for a splash of blood. There was no body. One or more of them had been close enough to retrieve the dead one.

Hanson looked at his hands, then glanced to his right to make sure none of the others was staring at him. He pushed his shaking, jittery hands deep into his trouser pockets and tried to spit over the wall, except he did not have enough saliva to work up a good spit.

The taste of gunpowder left his mouth and was replaced

by the coppery flavor of blood although he was not wounded.

He shivered and turned to go back to the latrine. He needed to take a piss. Bad.

✦ 31 ✦

"CORPORAL!"

"I'm busy here, Hanson. Can this wait?" Berrenton and Thames were bending over Trooper Beard. Their attention was not a matter of respect for the dead but of hope for the living. They were stripping his body of his ammunition pouches.

"Yeah, Corporal, I expect it can wait at that," Hanson mumbled to himself. He did what he'd gone back there for and returned to the wall.

When he looked out toward the Indians—completely out of sight again—there was something different. It took him a moment to recognize what was missing. The tripod holding Vickers's body upright had fallen down. Some of the savages must have jostled it during their mad dash against the wall of defenders or in their even more vigorous retreat after being repulsed. "Thank goodness for small favors," he said to himself.

"What?"

"Nothing, Ragen. Just nattering."

"Oh. All right." They stood in silence for a minute, then Ragen asked, "They'll come again, won't they, Hanson?"

"Yeah, buddy. They'll come again." It occurred to Hanson that he'd never before called any of the damnyankee

soldiers buddy or anything like it. Now it seemed natural
for him to do so. Ragen and Thames and Berrenton stood
firm in the face of fire. Hanson could not fault them, nor
could he hate them. He should, he supposed, quit thinking
of them as damnyankees and instead consider them to be
Yankees. And soldiers. They certainly were that.

Berrenton came over and gave Ragen and then Hanson
each seven rounds of carbine ammunition and three pistol
cartridges.

"Thanks."

"There was something you wanted to tell me, Hanson?"

"Yeah, Corporal, it's about—"

"Grüss Gott!" one of the Swiss bellowed. He started
screaming in German, and Berrenton forgot about Hanson
and ran over to the swarm of shouting, arm-waving, agitated Swiss.

"Funny," Hanson said, "I'd always heard squareheads
were about as excitable as so many lumps of suet. Kinda
looks like I was wrong about that, doesn't it?"

"I'll say it does." Ragen shook his head and turned his
attention back to Hanson, neither of them speaking any
German and having no idea what all the excitement was
over there. "Tell me something, Hanson."

"Mm?" Hanson leaned against the wall and kept his
eyes focused out onto the desert but his ears tuned to
Ragen.

"What d'you think our chances are here?"

Hanson looked at him and grinned. "Our chances of
achieving a great victory by killing more of them than
they kill of us? Or the chances that you and I personally
are gonna live to ride away from this place?"

"You know what I mean."

Hanson looked off across the desert again. They would
have had a chance if that relief column had been coming.
They really would have. "You sure you want me to tell
you, Albert?"

"No, maybe I don't at that. By the way, my friends mostly call me Al."

"Then Al it is." He grinned again. "And you can call me Sir."

Trooper Al Ragen laughed.

"Got any tobacco on you . . . sir?"

"Wish I did, Al, but that's a vice I never courted." His smile was easy and seemingly unworried. "I was always told, you see, that a man should hold one vice in reserve just so he can feel virtuous about himself while indulging in all the others. Tobacco is the vice I decided to forgo."

"Maybe Johnny had some on him. He—"

"Hanson! Ragen! Thames! Get your sorry asses over here and stand to attention. Do it *now*!"

"Yes, Corporal."

"Right away, Corporal."

"Yo."

Whatever this was about, Hanson was fairly sure he wasn't going to like it.

✣ 32 ✣

"NOW LISTEN UP, goddammit. Herr Schwartman tells me that a bag of their gold is missing. He checked the cart after the fight, and one bag is gone. Herr Schwartman and his people already own the stuff, so none of them would have any reason to steal it. Which leaves just us."

Berrenton turned and said something to the Swiss with the shotgun, who presumably was this Schwartman fellow. Not that Hanson knew or cared at this point which of them was who just so long as they could all shoot when those Indians came again.

To the squad members Berrenton said, "I'm gonna search you, then after I do that, I want each of you to stand over there where you can be watched by Herr Heuer and some of their people. You stand in plain sight, you hear me? Then Herr Schwartman will search through your personal effects. And let me tell whoever did this that charges *will* be filed when we get back to Camp Lune. You can count on that."

Hanson was pleased to hear the corporal refer to the time *when* they got back to Lune instead of *if*. A soldier's attitude can make a helluva difference when it comes time to fight, and Hanson liked Berrenton's.

"Permission to speak, Corporal?" He remained at rigid attention.

"What is it, Hanson?"

"With the corporal's permission, may I request that the personal gear of each trooper be searched by the corporal himself? It's a matter of military propriety and protocol, Corporal, them being foreign nationals and all."

"I thought you considered yourself to be a foreign national, Hanson."

"I gave my parole, Corporal, and I intend to honor it. Although, God willing, I would like to think I'll someday live in a free and sovereign Confederate States of America once more."

"What about you, Ragen? Thames? How do you feel about this?"

"I'm with Hanson, Corporal."

"Me, too. Except for that part about wanting t' live in the Confed'racy, that is," Ragen said with a smile.

"But you don't object to me conducting the search?"

"No, Corporal. There's nothing in my gear to be found."

"Mine neither."

"Nor mine."

Berrenton turned to the Swiss and spoke with them at length. "All right then," he said when that conversation was over. "I will do the searching. Herr Heuer will observe while I do so. Herr Schwartman will keep watch over you three."

"Permission to speak again, Corporal?"

"What is it this time, Hanson?"

"First, I don't mind being observed by any son of a bitch, but if that kraut-eating squarehead thinks he can hold a shotgun on me, he should know that I will take it away from him and run it down his damned throat. Not while I'm wearing this . . . or any other . . . uniform, he won't. Secondly, I think I know who stole that gold. I have no idea where it is, but I'm pretty sure I know who took it."

"And who would that be, Hanson?"

"Trooper Joseph, sir. During the fight when I was reaching for my cap pouch, I saw some movement over by the handcarts. It was Joseph, Corporal. I didn't see what he was doing there, but that's where he was."

"Come to think of it, dammit, where is that cowardly little peckerwood? I forgot clean about him, the useless little bastard." Berrenton scowled. He turned toward the cliff and bellowed, "Joseph! Front and center, damn you!"

"Corporal."

"What, Hanson?"

"He isn't going to come, Corporal."

"Now, why would you say that?"

"That's what I was trying to tell you before, Corporal. Trooper Joseph is dead. His body is back behind the horses. I saw it lying there when I went to take a leak a while ago."

"Jesus! If it isn't one thing it's another." Berrenton spoke to the Swiss again. Whatever he said was not to their liking, but it appeared that the corporal was in no humor for argument at this point.

He aimed a finger at Thames and then at Ragen. "You. And you. Over there. And don't touch anything. Don't go anyplace. Don't even scratch yourselves. I'll be back in a minute, and we'll do this search crap. You." He pointed at Hanson. "Show me. You." He pointed at Heuer and snapped something curt and angry at him, too.

With a sigh, Hanson headed off toward the latrine area.

✠ 33 ✠

IT WAS ENTIRELY too clear how Nathan Joseph died. He'd stuck the muzzle of his Colt into his mouth and pressed the trigger. The result was messy.

Hanson remembered thinking that when the time came, Joseph would have to decide whether to fight or to die. His choice was quite frankly surprising. And one that Hanson himself was unable to comprehend. How a man could take his own life. . . . Oh, maybe if he were in actual, imminent danger of being captured by the Indians and killed the way poor Vickers died.

But . . . this? They had a strong, fortified position here. The Indians might wear them down and defeat them through attrition. Or the men could well perish or become too weak to fight through lack of water—a greater likelihood to Hanson's mind than defeat in battle—but . . . this? He did not understand the sort of fear that must have twisted poor Joseph's gut to drive him to this extreme.

"See if the gold is on him, Hanson."

"Yes, Corporal." The task was damned well distasteful because it involved looking into the pockets of a body that had voided itself of both urine and feces upon death. At least there had been time enough for most of it to dry.

Hanson stripped Joseph's equipment belt off and

checked the pouches. Berrenton did not give him any instruction about that, so Hanson appropriated Joseph's ammunition for himself. The poor, sad, cowardly soul had fired scarcely a round since they got here. He had nearly his full issue of both carbine and pistol ammunition intact.

There was no gold in the pouches though.

Rather than reach inside Joseph's pockets—there was no spare water that he could have washed his hands with afterward, and that fact bothered him—Hanson settled for picking up a stout twig and using that to press the cloth flat over Joseph's pockets.

"There's nothing lumpy, Corporal. No bag of gold here. Looks like a pocket knife and something small like maybe a pair of dice, but no bag of gold."

Heuer spoke, and Berrenton answered him. They appeared to argue a little, although nothing too hot. Eventually Berrenton snapped something at the Swiss, and Heuer stepped forward to bend over Joseph's body. The Swiss obviously felt no reluctance to soil his hands. He flopped the corpse onto its side and stuck his hand into that pocket, turned it over and reached into the pocket on the other side, too. He brought out only a pocket knife and a carved charm of some sort, the object Hanson had thought was a pair of dice.

But Heuer found no gold on the body.

In a spate of anger and frustration, the Swiss kicked Joseph's thigh.

Hanson started for him, but Corporal Berrenton got there first. Berrenton grabbed Heuer by the shirt and yanked him close so the two were eyeball to eyeball. Hanson could not understand the words that Berrenton snarled, but he did not have to. He understood that tone of voice quite well.

Heuer became flushed, but with embarrassment rather than anger. He apologized profusely. Again Hanson did not need the language to understand what was being said.

The man's action was understandable enough, Hanson thought. But inexcusable regardless.

Berrenton and Heuer spoke again, calmly and with careful politeness, and the Swiss returned to the front where his friends were waiting.

"You and me will drag Joseph back there and cover him over," the corporal said. "Get his hands. I'll take the feet."

They deposited the body beside Michael Kelly's and scooped some gravel over it. Hanson was more interested in covering Kelly than Joseph though, because Kelly had been dead long enough to bloat and stink. That end of the redoubt was hardly a pleasant place to visit.

When they were done, Hanson headed in the direction of the wall, but Berrenton stopped him with a touch on the elbow.

"Tell me something, Johnny Reb."

"Yes, Corporal?"

"You didn't really see Joseph come close enough to the fighting to take something out of that handcart, did you?"

Hanson only smiled.

"Yeah, well, you did the right thing. Thanks."

They returned to the front where the Swiss and the two troopers were still unhappily facing each other.

✛ 34 ✛

THE SWISS QUITE sensibly insisted that the remaining men and the personal gear of both living and dead be searched. Berrenton did the searching, slow and thorough about it. He found nothing and spoke at some length with both Heuer and Schwartman.

Hanson had the impression that the Swiss wanted to search again and this time do it themselves. Berrenton did not let them.

The civilians accepted the situation, but any hint of camaraderie in the face of a common enemy had been shattered rather completely. The Swiss dragged the handcart containing the rest of their gold over to the far right of the wall where Berrenton's post had been.

They chose to occupy the right half of the defense while the cavalrymen, four of them still living while there were now seven Swiss, took responsibility for the left.

"You really think they'll come again?" Ragen asked along about the middle of the afternoon.

"Count on it," Hanson told him. Not that he really knew how a savage might choose to fight. But it was better to be prepared than not, so yes was the answer best suited now.

"Hanson."

"Yo, Corporal?"

"You took Joseph's ammunition, didn't you?"

"Yes, Corporal."

"Share it out with the rest of us."

"Right, Corporal." He gave each of the others eight rounds of Sharps ammo and kept a dozen for himself while conveniently forgetting about the pistol cartridges. He also had Joseph's Colt stuffed into his belt, fully charged except for the one round Joseph had expended on himself.

It was not that Hanson did not trust the fighting abilities of the Yankees . . . just that he trusted himself more.

"You really think they'll come, do you?"

"Yes, Al," Hanson told him patiently. "I really do."

✠ 35 ✠

ONE OF THE Swiss let out a loud, startled yelp. Hanson looked that way in time to see an Indian—just a damn kid really, twelve or thirteen years old maybe—come racing along the front side of the wall so close he probably scraped his left shoulder on his way past.

Little bastard was quick, and that was the truth. He was past the Swiss, past Berrenton and Thames and Ragen and smack in front of Hanson before anybody had time enough to react.

Without particularly thinking it through, Hanson reached out to grab him. He got a handful of hair and pulled, but the kid was running full speed and hardly slowed. He tossed his head and ripped the hank of hair loose from Hanson's grasp and kept on running along the base of the mesa.

Hanson snatched Joseph's Colt from his waistband and leveled it at the kid's back.

The revolver was loaded and cocked and Hanson had a steady aim on the base of the boy's spine. The kid was for all practical purposes dead and starting to rot.

Except Hanson didn't pull the trigger.

There was no excuse for that. Really there wasn't. It didn't matter a lick that the boy was only a scrawny, nearly naked kid barely out of diapers . . . or whatever a bunch of savages used instead of diapers. No excuse at all.

But he didn't pull the damned trigger, and in a blink of an eye it was too late to change his mind. The boy disappeared behind a jagged boulder and was gone.

"What the hell happened?"

"He hit me. The li'l son'a'bish hit me wid stick. Dem stick wid fedders on't."

"Hit you with a stick?"

"Ja. Wid fedders."

Berrenton frowned, then said something in German.

"Ja. Fedders."

"Feathers."

"I say dot. Fedders."

"Right."

It seemed that Hanson's pal Gerd the butcher could speak English. Badly, but speak it he could. Not that Hanson could blame them for trying to keep that a secret. He supposed the idea was so Gerd could listen in if the Americans got to talking about how they should divvy up the Swiss gents' gold. Or whatever.

Gerd held his hands about two and a half feet apart. "Stick, I telt to you. Dis big, ja. Big aroun' lak dis finner." He held up his pinky to demonstrate. "Hit me. Here." He pointed to his right shoulder. "Coulda shoot me. Coulda poke me. He hit me. Wid dat dem stick wid da fedders on't." Gerd shook his head. "Dem dummkopf kid."

"Brave little bastard," Thames said.

"Showing off," Hanson suggested. "Maybe you got it right, Chris. Maybe he was showing his pals how brave he is."

"You could of shot him, Reb . . . sir," Ragen said.

"Naw," he lied. "Couldn't get a bead on him. He was just a hair too quick for me."

"Yeah, he was fast, all right."

"Brave, too," Thames repeated.

"Let's just hope they all aren't that brave," Berrenton said. He turned to Gerd. "I see you found your English, mister."

The butcher shrugged and gave the Americans a sheepish half grin. Didn't apologize for the deception, though. Which seemed fair enough to Hanson.

Dammit though, he should have shot that little son of a bitch when he had the chance.

And what in hell, he wondered, was this stuff about running right up to them with a stick in his hand and whacking one of them with it, then running away without shooting or anything?

Weird, that was all. These damned savages were truly and totally strange.

He fooled with Joseph's Colt for a moment, revolving the cylinder until a spent chamber was under the hammer again and a fresh one ready to rotate into position the next time the piece was cocked.

He began to think about supper, too. Berrenton's horse was bloating and starting to smell bad by now. He wondered if they should go ahead and butcher the horse with the arrow in its hip. He decided he would take a look at the wound. If it was festering, the animal was useless anyway, so they might as well take the blood for the moisture that would provide and the meat to supply their needs for the next couple days.

He'd bring that up to Berrenton, he decided. But only if the arrow wound was festering.

Crazy damned kid. But like Thames said . . . brave.

Hanson leaned his carbine against the base of the wall—if they were going to have Indians wandering around all that close, he didn't want to leave it where one of them could reach over and take it—and went to look at the horse while there was still some daylight left.

✦ 36 ✦

IF—BIG IF—if he survived this patrol and could look back on it years and years in the future, there were two things he expected to remember. Well, the Indians and the fighting and all that, too, of course. But really there were two things that he knew would never leave him. One was the stink. Lord, but this place reeked of dead things. The other was the flies. He swore that every fly between Texas and California had to have heard about the free lunch laid out here, and every damn one of them had come to join the party.

He stood, his back aching from maintaining a stooped, bent-over posture for too long a time, and called out, "Anybody that's thirsty better come now before this stuff starts to coagulate."

Gerd added to the invitation in German, and all the Swiss hurried over to get their share of the warm, coppery, vile tasting but liquid and therefore life-giving blood. Hanson drank down his share, and Ragen came to have some, too. Thames and Berrenton did not.

"You better do this while you can," Hanson advised them.

"No thanks." Thames shook his head but kept his attention—or at least his eyes—focused out onto the desert.

"Corporal?"

Berrenton frowned. But he came back to where Hanson and Gerd had carried the pot and ladle. The corporal took the ladle, hesitated, and then drank a little. Quickly he shoved the ladle back into Gerd's hands and whirled around, bending over and retching until there was nothing left to come up.

"God, that's awful."

"Nobody ever said it was good, just that it's good for you. Keep you alive, Corporal. There's something can be said for that, y'know."

"If anything's gonna keep me alive, Hanson, it will be my carbine and pistol. Nothing else."

"Whatever you say, Corporal."

Among them they emptied the pot and a smaller one as well, then Hanson and Gerd Wolfe went back to concentrate on turning as much of the horse into meat as they could manage.

The defenders might not have much to drink, but they were in no danger of running out of food.

The big question at this point was who would get to eat all these steaks they were cooking and all the strips they were drying: the defenders or the damned savages who were out there howling and dancing once more.

On the other hand, better the Indians should cavort around a bonfire than make the attack Hanson had been expecting all afternoon.

Hell, if that's what they wanted, he would be willing to personally carry wood to keep their fire burning.

He wiped some sweat off his forehead, rubbed at the painful gall in his left armpit . . . and went back to slicing horsemeat into strips.

"STAND EASY NOW, boys, but keep your eyes open. I'm leaving you two to keep watch for a few minutes. I need t' talk with Hanson in private."

He could hear Berrenton's whisper, and a moment later the corporal stopped in front of him. "This way, Trooper." Berrenton inclined his head toward the charnel house at the back of the redoubt.

Over toward the other wall, Hanson could faintly see movement. One of the Swiss, no doubt, keeping track of the Americans. Just in case . . . but then who knew what they could be worried about. In case of another theft attempt. In case the soldiers decided to slip away in the night. Whatever.

Berrenton led him behind the horses, which stirred and nosed at him likely in search of water and grain.

"God, I wish I had something to give them."

"So do I, Corporal. So do I."

Berrenton glanced toward the place where the Swiss had bedded down while the troopers stood the first watch, then tilted his head and looked up at Hanson, who was uncommonly tall for a cavalryman, most cav troopers being sawed-off examples of soldiery. But then for the sake of the horses 140 pounds was the absolute upper weight limit for a cavalryman and 120 to 125 the norm. When the U.S. Army weighed Hanson, he was 128 exactly. By now he was back to his preprison weight of 150 or so.

"D'you mind a question, Hanson?"

"Go ahead."

"Before . . . you weren't a private then, were you?"

Hanson hesitated. This was not something he really wanted to get into. He'd promised himself he would not. After all, those days were gone and now best buried deep in his memory until this war was over. "I wasn't a private then, Corporal. But I am now. Can we leave it at that please?"

"All right. I just kind of thought maybe that was the case. Truth is, knowing it makes me feel a little better about coming to you for advice like I been doing."

"You're doing fine, Corporal. You're a good soldier."

"Thanks. I mean that. Thank you. But I got to tell you, I'm worried and more than just a little. We're in a bad situation here. It would be all right if the troop was coming. But they aren't. They got no idea where we are or that we need help."

"No, we're on our own, that's true enough. And in a helluva squeeze."

"Hanson, if you was in charge . . . and you're not, of course, nor will you be . . . but if you was in charge, what would you do?"

"I expect I'd do pretty much the same as you, Corporal. Stand firm and hold the Indians off as long as we can. Hope they got better things to do than risk dying just to take a few more white scalps."

"What I've been wondering is if I should make another try to alert the lieutenant. Get the troop on their way here."

"Send another rider, you mean."

"That's right. I been thinking about it all afternoon. Seeing Vickers hanging on that tripod this morning . . .

God, was that just this morning? It seems like a week at the least."

"It's been a full day, Corporal."

"Hasn't it just." Berrenton squatted so he could see underneath the bellies of the horses and looked toward the Swiss again. One of them was sitting up with a blanket around his shoulders.

Hanson guessed some or even all of the other Swiss were also awake. They were not very trustful companions. But they could shoot. Right now, marksmanship was more important than brotherly love.

Berrenton stood again and squinted at the tall reb. "Would you volunteer if I asked for a rider?"

Hanson shook his head. "It would be suicide, Corporal."

"You think so?"

"I'm certain of it. Yesterday I think you could've done that. Before that new bunch arrived. Best of all last night while they were out there having so much fun torturing poor Vickers. Hell, to tell you the God's truth, I thought about taking off on my own.

"But it couldn't be done now. Apart from there being twice as many Indians out there as there were to begin with, these horses aren't up to it any longer. They've been short of water pretty much since we left that *rancheria* back east of here. I noticed it in that blood we took this afternoon. It's thick and sticky and dark, Corporal. They've lost moisture. Even if we chose one horse and gave it all the water we have left among us, it's too late to do any good. It would take those animals days, prob'ly a week, to get their strength back even if we had all the grain and water they need.

"Send a rider out on a horse like that and he might as well be on foot. Come to think of it, the Indians would hear and chase a man on horseback. A man on foot just might get past them. But the only thing he'd accomplish would be to save himself. There's no way a man could walk back to Camp Lune and bring help in time for it to do any good. The rest would be dead before the troop could get here." Hanson scratched himself. Lord, what wouldn't he give for a cool bath right now. He was sticky with sweat and dried blood after the fighting and the butchering, and his clothes felt like they were full of creeping, crawling lice. For that matter, they probably were. He didn't want to look to see.

"I suppose you could turn the squad loose to sneak out afoot one by one, every man for himself and the devil take the hindmost."

"Would you do that, Hanson?"

"No, Corporal, I guess I would not if the call were mine to make. Differences aside, Jesse . . . D'you mind if I call you Jesse? Differences aside, we're professional soldiers. It's our job to defend civilians like those squareheads, and it has nothing to do with their gold. I expect if they'd been willing to abandon that, they could've been out of here free and clear themselves before we ever came onto them. They didn't do that, and now it's up to us to pull their fat out of the fire." He smiled. "Or die in the attempt. That is something professional soldiers do, too."

Berrenton sighed. "Whatever I decide, men are going to die."

"Dying is something every man has to do sooner or later, Jesse. It's how you live that matters."

"Better get back to your post, Trooper Hanson."

"Aye, Corporal." He adjusted his hat and came to attention, saluted, and executed a snappy about-face. It was a matter of respect. He hoped Berrenton understood that. Even if he was a damnyankee.

✦ 38 ✦

DAWN WAS A magical time of day. Hanson had always thought that. Each dawning held the promise of all the wondrous things that could happen and held, too, the mystery of the many as yet unknown things that would happen. Every dawn was special, he thought, and these desert dawnings were perhaps the finest of them all.

There was a clarity in the air that made images sharper than seemed possible. As light infused the eastern sky and colors began to form, they were vivid beyond belief.

The desert skies were often perfectly cloudless, as they were on this morning, and for reasons he could not begin to understand, well before that first golden break of day, all sound and motion paused as if to pay homage to the day that was borning. The night breezes subsided and then disappeared altogether. The flutter of unseen wings from the night hunting birds ceased, and the scrabble of tiny claws ended as the nocturnal creatures tucked themselves out of sight for another day.

The air was chill and clean and tasted like mountain spring water.

Mountain spring water. God, what would he give for a cup of water frigid from the ground. He could practically feel it on his tongue and deep in his throat. Hanson found himself swallowing involuntarily just at the thought of cold water.

At that *rancheria* the farmer—rancher, dammit, they were called ranchers here—the man Hartford was blessed to have water in such abundance. Hanson hoped the man knew how fortunate he was.

Somewhere to the left, one of the odd little desert quail whistled. So very different from the call of the bobwhite, and—

"Shit!"

"What's the matter?"

"Everybody get ready. I think that bird call could've been an Indian making like a quail. I think they might be coming again."

Berrenton passed the warning all in German for the benefit of the Swiss, and up and down the thin, stubborn line, Hanson could hear the sound of locks being cocked and throats cleared.

"You sure 'bout this, Reb?" Ragen asked. His voice was steady and he sounded more interested than alarmed.

"No, I'm not at all sure, Al." Hanson smiled. "But I expect I'd rather be wrong than be surprised."

"You do have a point there."

"I be glad dey no Injun out dere no more, none," Gerd put in from over on the right. He laughed and said something to his companions, probably repeating the unlikely but highly appealing wish.

Another quail called on the far right.

"Is that what you're hearing, Hanson?"

"Yes 'tis, Corporal."

"Sounds like they're up to something on our flanks, doesn't it," Berrenton observed. "Hanson, Ragen, you two ignore whatever happens out in front. They may put on a display to divert our attention. You two defend the left flank. Herr Heuer . . ." Hanson assumed the corporal was passing on a similar order for the Swiss to assign two or three of their people to the right flank.

Goodness but a bucket of cold spring water would be nice about now, Hanson thought. He would drink half of it and bathe in the rest. And then probably drink that, too.

A thunder of hoofs broke the morning stillness, and well out on the desert the savages began to shriek.

Hanson saw nothing of that charge, however. He leaned over the sights of his carbine and waited for the real attack to begin.

TWO, THREE, FOUR of them. Rushing fast and silent from around the scattered boulders at the base of the cliff. They carried hatchets. Tomahawks, he supposed those would be called, even though they looked like ordinary framing hatchets. The thought of what a framing hatchet could do to a man's skull . . .

Hanson was able to think about such things even as eye and muscle and much too much practice took over to do what needed to be done. He had never been sure if it was this sense of calm that allowed him to kill his enemies without compunction or if it was the mind-sharpening effects of combat that gave him a sense of detachment to begin with. Chicken or egg.

Not that it mattered.

What did matter was that his aim was good and his hands sure.

"Now, Al," he said in an easy, conversational tone of voice even as his right index finger closed gently on the trigger of his Sharps.

The little gun barked and rocked in his hands, and fifteen yards away, the leading warrior's head was wreathed in a spray of glistening red gore and the front of the man's face collapsed in on itself. Hanson would have shot the last in line first had he wanted to be sure of taking them all down, but his goal at the moment was not to kill four Indians but to stop the charge. And God knew how many more of them were poised to follow this first deadly rush.

Ragen fired, too, and the next Indian in line was hit high on the left side of his chest, the impact of the ball spinning him half around and causing him to lose his balance and fall sprawling onto the stones and gravel.

Hanson set the carbine down and picked up his revolver. He fired, missed with it, fired again. Indian number three cried out in sudden pain—so much for silent stoicism—and turned to go at a hard limp back the way he'd just come. Hanson thought he'd hit the warrior in the hip, but he was not sure.

The fourth warrior tried to press the fight alone. Both Hanson and Ragen fired at virtually the same time, their pistol shots raising small, moist dimples in the flesh on his belly.

Half a dozen more Indians came shrieking out of the boulders, hurling insults and arrows, but instead of rushing the wall, they came only as far as their wounded companions, grabbed them, and immediately retreated, leaving the one Indian with only half his head still on the ground.

"Al." He had to speak loudly to be heard above the roar of the fighting as other defenders met the charge on the front.

"Yes, sir?" He did not sound like he was teasing a fellow trooper when he used the word this time.

"I'm betting they'll break toward us again and try to get that dead one. It's just a hunch, but let's you and me let 'em do that. D'you hear? Don't fire unless they come past the dead one. If they do that, use your pistol and give them a look at Hell from the inside, all right?"

"You sure about that?"

"No, I'm not sure, Al. But my gut tells me it's best."

"All right. All right then. But if they come one inch closer . . ."

"You and me both, buddy."

The Indians came, the same half dozen as before or a matching set for those, rushing out of the boulders at a run.

"Their hands are empty, Al. No weapons. Hold your fire."

Ragen said nothing. But he did not shoot, either.

The savages grabbed their fallen comrade and ran with the body toward the safety of the boulders, all but one of them who stood upright and defiant for half a heartbeat staring back at the white defenders who were watching him over the sights of their revolvers. After an instant, he let out a chilling yelp and spun to race after the others.

The field was clear of bodies, living and dead.

"We coulda shot him, sir."

"Yes, and maybe should've. Too late to worry about now." He glanced to the front, thinking perhaps Ragen should join the fighting in that direction while he maintained his watch on the flank.

There was no need. The mounted charge from the front had broken and turned also, leaving the defenders agitated but unharmed. Hanson stepped back a pace and looked along the line. No one was dead, no one wounded.

"Bastards," Thames grumbled.

"Isn't that the natural truth."

"Shut your yaps and check your pieces," Berrenton snapped. "Make sure you're reloaded and ready for the next time."

Hanson felt vaguely ashamed of himself to realize that the corporal had to remind him about something so basic. He hadn't yet reloaded his carbine and hurried to do so now.

So far, though, so good. He was just hoping that the defenders wanted to live more than the Indians wanted to kill them. Because if the Indians stayed where they were and continued to press the siege, they would inevitably triumph. Damn them.

Hanson tossed the flash-paper tail of the fresh cartridge aside and fitted a musket cap onto the nipple of the Sharps, then set it down and began the much slower task of recharging the .44 caliber Colt revolver.

✧ 40 ✧

"JESUS, YOU DON'T think that was the object of the assault, do you?" Ragen asked of no one in particular. The four American cavalrymen and seven remaining Swiss were all staring toward the back of the redoubt.

Flights of arrows had swept high over the wall during the dawn charge and landed among the horses hobbled near the rear of the fortified notch in the mesa wall. The last of the horses was down and dying now.

"Dammit!" Berrenton scowled and spat.

Hanson only sighed. He nodded toward the Swiss, gathered in a cluster at the right of the defensive line, and said, "Come on, Gerd, we'd best salvage what blood and meat we can. There won't be any more once this spoils."

They should, he thought, dry as much of the horsemeat as possible. They had some dried meat from the butchering they'd done already. But there were eleven men here all needing rations and now only horsemeat to supply those needs. The desiccated soup the Swiss carried was worthless without some form of liquid to mix it with. He wondered briefly if they should try to capture fluids from the newly dead horses' kidneys . . . then concluded that might not be such a very good idea.

But in another few days, their lack of water would become critical. Men turn lethargic and incapacitated and soon die if they cannot consume the fluids they need. Hanson had seen it on battlefields where men lay wounded for several days crying out for water and succumbing quickly to injuries that did not seem all that serious to begin with.

Hanson still had a little water left in his canteen.

But not enough to share with ten other men.

Best to let no one know, he decided, rather than try to pick and choose.

He and Gerd took out their knives and started back toward the carcasses of the recently killed horses.

✢ 41 ✢

THE BLOODY, STICKY, stinking work was interrupted after an hour or so by a great hubbub from the Swiss.

Gerd muttered a "Dem't," which Hanson took to mean damn it, and ran to join his companions. Hanson followed more slowly.

Once again the Swiss were facing down the Americans with leveled weapons. This time Berrenton had his revolver out, too, while Ragen and Thames, looking thoroughly confused, held their carbines.

Heuer was shouting something, and Schwartman was brandishing a poke of gold aloft as if it had some significance, while Berrenton was shouting back at Heuer in an excited, stumbling German.

Rather than go over and join the other troopers, Hanson sidled over behind the Swiss, a position that Berrenton noticed but that did not seem to alarm the Swiss. Karl even glanced back toward him with a satisfied nod, perhaps assuming this meant he took Hanson's position to indicate that he was taking sides with the Swiss. In fact, Hanson's intent was to place himself where they could put the German speakers in a crossfire if the foreigners wanted to escalate this into a gunfight . . . whatever *this* was.

After several testy minutes, the shouting slowed, and Berrenton told his men, "They've found the missing bag of gold, boys. It was buried in the sand over there at the right end of the wall. One of them uncovered it while he was scuffing his feet or something. I'm not real clear about that. Point is, they found it, and it's got them all stirred up again. Now they think we're all thieves, all in on this together."

"Crazy squarehead bastards," Ragen snorted.

"Tell them we'll be glad to fight it out with them," Thames said, "but not till after those damn Injuns leave."

Berrenton looked past the Swiss toward Hanson, who only shrugged and rolled his eyes.

What was done was done. It wouldn't matter a lick, if they all died here at the hands of the Indians.

Hanson left Berrenton jawing in German while Ragen and Thames went back to the wall to stand watch. A couple of the Swiss returned to the wall, too, and gave their attention to the matters at hand. With that many guns on the wall, Hanson returned to the dead horses and the chore of converting their flesh into dried meat.

There was not much wood remaining inside the redoubt, he noticed, so they wouldn't even be able to cook much of the fresh meat and preserve it for a little while that way. But then they might as well burn the saddles, too. That would help.

So would a bath.

He unbuttoned the dark blue woolen blouse and reached inside to scratch his armpit.

HANSON AND GERD were distributing thick steaks—army saddles did indeed burn quite nicely—when a half dozen riders came slowly out of the Indian encampment and stopped two hundred yards or so in front.

"I can bust one of them from here, Corporal," Ragen said. "You want I should shoot?"

The Indians sat there for several minutes in plain sight while Berrenton and the others stared at them. Berrenton spat across the wall. "No," he said, "not yet. I dunno what they're doing out there, but they could be wanting to talk. Could be a peace delegation, something like that."

"I don't see no white flag," Thames put in.

"Hell, for all I know Injuns don't understand white flags. But it looks like they got something on their minds. Wait a minute, they're moving. Hold your fire, boys, and let's see what they're up to." He repeated the admonition in German as well. "Hold your fire, but be ready," Berrenton ordered.

Hanson set aside the steaks piled on a square of saddle leather and went to his place on the line. He checked the caps on his revolver and carbine alike and dropped the pistol back into his holster but left the flap unsnapped. He leaned on the wall and picked up the carbine.

It occurred to him that when the squad made their dash inside the wall, their horses were able to easily jump the low sections. He could not see why Indian ponies would not be able to do the same thing if the savages wanted to press a direct assault and try to get inside the defenses.

Not that there was much of anything they could do about it at this point. But it was something to keep in mind. Perhaps he should suggest to Berrenton that they build up those low spots, try to make the entire wall too tall for a horse to jump. Or they could—

"Here they come, boys! Remember now. Hold your fire. I want to see what they're up to."

The six riders had curved around to the right, stopping about a hundred yards beyond Heuer, who was anchoring the Swiss end of the line.

Now they started toward the wall but not in a bunch as if preparing an assault. One rider came forward at a trot, picking his gait up to a canter after a few moments and at about that same time another single rider trotted forward and then gigged his pony into a canter.

They came on one at a time with perhaps ten yards between them.

"Hold fire now; hold fire."

"What the hell are they doing?"

"I dunno, but, geez boys, they're children. They're a bunch of damn children," Berrenton said.

It was true. They looked like they were not more than twelve or thirteen years old. Hanson thought he recognized the foremost of them from that bloodless pass he'd made the previous day.

"They aren't going to shoot," he guessed aloud. "This is another one of those showoff things, I'd bet. Proving how brave they are."

"Let them if that's what they want to do," Berrenton said.

Heuer said something, and Berrenton translated, "No weapons. They got no weapons on them."

As they came near, the boys brandished feathered sticks, but not a one of them appeared to have so much as a pocket knife as an offensive weapon.

The leading rider leaned low over the neck of his pony as he reached the wall. He slowed it to a rocking chair canter and held the feathered end of his stick out toward the defenders. He tried to tap Heuer on the head, but the Swiss pulled back away from the stick with a loud and obviously unhappy oath.

The boy shook his stick in the general direction of each of the defenders.

All but Hanson moved out of reach.

Hanson, for reasons that he himself did not completely understand, drew himself to attention and held his carbine at port arms. Acknowledging the child's bravery was what it amounted to. The kid could not have been more than twelve, and it looked like he was leading a bunch of his buddies in this show of bravado. Well, let him. Hanson would willingly kill the boy's father and every other adult male savage within a hundred miles. But he would rather not make war on children if he could help it.

The boy saw and his eyes widened as his pony reached Hanson. He lightly touched Hanson on the right shoulder and moved on.

Behind him the other boys saw and did the same, one by one, until all six had come past close enough to the wall for them to kick it with their moccasins if they wished.

That behavior was odd enough. Odder still was the fact that only the first four touched Hanson with their sticks. The last two in line tried instead to tap Ragen, who ducked away from them, and ignored Hanson, who continued to stand where he was.

"Crazy damn bunch, aren't they," Thames said to no

one in particular as the children were loping back to their lines.

"Wait a minute. Here's one more coming."

From the same direction to the right of the redoubt came one more horse, this one with paint streaked on its chest and hindquarters and its face painted with vermillion.

"This one's no damned kid," Berrenton said.

The rider, his face painted much like that of the horse and his naked chest streaked with white and black stripes, carried a lance with a tuft of feathers at the business end. The feathers failed to hide the fact that the lance was tipped with a very wicked looking splinter of sharpened steel.

"You think this one just wants to show off how brave he is, too?" Thames asked.

"Who the hell cares? Shoot the son of a bitch."

When the rider reached the wall, he was greeted with a sheet of flame as several of the Swiss and all of the Americans fired.

The painted pony shied away from the flame and smoke and raced back toward the Indian positions, leaving its rider's body bloody and tattered on the ground outside the wall.

"Aw, hell," Berrenton mumbled. "We should've waited until he was farther away before we shot him. Now they're gonna charge us again so they can get the bastard's body back."

"You really think so?"

"Count on it, an' if it don't happen be glad. But I'm betting they'll come. Dammit!"

✢ 43 ✢

THE ATTACK DID not come. The afternoon wore slowly on, a blanket of heat lying on the sun-baked desert to discourage movement. The only visible motion came from a quartet of vultures that soared effortlessly overhead.

"If I had about five more cartridges," Thames grumbled, "I'd shoot one of those sons of bitches. I swear, I hate those birds about as bad as I hate Injuns."

"That's right, Chris. Damn redskin might kill you, but at least he won't eat you afterward."

Thames shivered. "Gives me the jibberty-wups just thinking about it."

Hanson put it, "There's a way to avoid becoming buzzard bait. Just make sure it's the Indians that get killed here, not you."

"D'you think those birds will come dig at the boys back there?" Thames pointed with his chin toward the back of the notch where the dead were laid out and so thinly covered.

"No," Hanson lied. "It's too confined for them to come in." He neglected to mention that smaller creatures were already eating the dead, human and horse alike. But then the stink of their rotting was high enough to attract carrion eaters for dozens of miles in every direction.

The smell was bad and getting worse. He hated having to smell it when he breathed in. But the alternative, to breathe through his mouth, seemed somehow even worse. It was foolish to think there could be anything in the air that would get onto his tongue or in his mouth. But he did not want to do it anyway. The thought was as repugnant to him as that of being eaten by buzzards seemed to be to Trooper Thames.

The good thing, he realized, was that in this dry, dry land, the bloat and the smell would very soon subside. The bodies would lose moisture and begin to shrink and soon—he was not sure exactly how long to expect before this relief—they would begin to take on the leathery appearance of a mummy.

When he was a boy, Hanson actually saw a mummy once. Or so the owner of the traveling show said it was. It had been dark and wrinkled and the eye holes were empty sockets, the yellowed teeth exposed in a ghastly, lipless grimace. He had seen very similar corpses on old battlefields back East. Funny thing though, despite all the intervening years, he could recall the sight of that ancient mummy much more clearly than any of the battlefield dead.

That was one of the educational benefits of warfare, he reflected now. A man became so very well acquainted with death and its aftermath.

"Anybody want a steak?" he asked loudly enough for all to hear. "These last weren't cooked too thoroughly, and I'm afraid they'll spoil if we don't eat them this afternoon."

✝ 44 ✝

THE NIGHT WAS long and nervous. The damned Indians kept parading back and forth with pitch-pine torches on some unknown errands or rituals. The effect of the torchlight was mesmerizing. And more than a little worrisome. The savages had something in mind, and none of the defenders had the least idea what it might be.

The Swiss took the early watch, but Hanson and the other troopers did not even try to sleep immediately. Not with those flickering, maddening torches moving to and fro on the desert.

Eventually, Hanson grunted and said, "You boys stay up all night if you like. Me, I'm going to bed." Lordy, he wished he *could* go to an actual bed. Inside an actual house. After a bath and a long, refreshing drink of water. Or milk. Jesus, milk cool from the springhouse with that rich, almost smoky flavor it had before the butter was taken from it. Or buttermilk with salt and pepper stirred into it. Or . . . or damn near anything that was wet and wouldn't poison a man.

Hanson sat on his blanket and debated with himself. Should he have a swallow of precious water now? Or wait a little longer? Willpower and bodily need warred within him. In the end he settled for moistening his lips with the most meager of sips and holding that half teaspoon full of fluid in his mouth until he could stand it no longer.

Then he lay down and immediately dropped into sleep.

"Heinz!" The cry was anguished and piercing.

Hanson came onto his feet before he was conscious of waking, carbine already in hand. He stumbled to the wall to find Berrenton already there and the Swiss in an uproar. Thames hurried to his place, and Ragen followed, puffy-eyed and disheveled.

"What the hell is going on over there?" Thames grumbled.

"Christ!" Berrenton blurted after he sorted out the torrents of excited German coming from the Swiss end of the line. "Heinz Mann is dead."

"Who?"

"The one with the red shirt."

"Oh yeah, him. What happened?"

"Son of a bitch has one of those tomahawk things buried in the front of his skull."

"But how . . . ?"

"Damn Injuns snuck in close. They must've done it while we were all awake, too. What d'you bet? Must've been while we were all so busy watching the torches that we never paid any mind to what was going on right under our noses," Berrenton said.

"And what do you bet the body of that dead one has been recovered?" Hanson added. "Bastards make it a point to retrieve their dead and wounded, don't they?" There had been times—all too many times—when he'd wished white commanders on both sides of the battle line cared and did as much for the unfortunates who were cut down on the field. He'd seen fights when the wounded languished in agony for two, even three days and nights before death gave them mercy and ended their cries. Civ-

ilized men did that to one another, but these painted savages did not. Amazing.

Berrenton went off and talked to the Swiss once things
calmed down a little at that end of the line. When he came
back, he said, "They say Mann was leaning on the wall.
They thought he was dozing. Then Karl Bauer asked him
something, and when Mann didn't answer gave him a
nudge to wake him up. Mann's body fell down. That's
the first any of them knew anything was wrong."

"They didn't even hear the hatchet hit? Damn, Corporal, it must've sounded like a punkin being whacked."

"Nobody noticed."

"Were all the useless bastards asleep on guard?"
Thames said.

Gerd, who seemed to understand more English than he
could speak, overheard and repeated it for his companions. That got the Swiss stirred up again, and they began
shouting insults back at the Americans, although only
Jesse Berrenton had any idea what they were saying.
Which, Hanson thought, was probably just as well.

Berrenton snapped back at the Swiss, then turned to his
men and ordered, "We'll have no more of that. Not from
any of you. Do you hear me? You better. We're all in
this together, and we'll not be fighting among ourselves.
Not as long as those Indians are out there. Am I making
myself clear?"

"Yes, Corporal."

"Yes, Corporal."

"Aye."

"All right then. Now settle down and pay attention to
what's going on in front of us. We don't want anybody
else winding up with a tomahawk for a hat."

"Yes, sir."

Over on the right, the still very agitated Swiss carried
Mann's body to the rear.

The dead, Hanson thought, were beginning to outnum-
ber the living.

✦ 45 ✦

DAYBREAK CAME AND went without incident. It also showed that, as Hanson had expected, the Indian they'd killed the day before was gone now, carried off at some time during the night.

Out on the desert the savages had another bonfire burning. They usually made fires that were virtually smoke free, but this time they laid greasewood or some similar combustible on to produce a plume of charcoal-gray smoke. The smoke rose several hundred feet before the lightly moving air caused it to dissipate.

"D'you think that's some sort o' funeral thing?" Ragen asked.

"Looks to me more like a signal," Berrenton said. "Could be there'll be more of them coming in."

"Thank goodness for that," Thames said.

"You say . . ."

"Yeah. It'd be a damn shame to run outa targets now that they finally got me riled up and wanting to shoot somebody."

The others got a chuckle out of that, and over on the Swiss side of things, Gerd translated the crack, and the Swiss started their day on a lighter note, too.

"Who's for a nice, thick steak for breakfast?"

"You and your horsemeat, Hanson. Do you get paid extra for cook duties or something?"

"Uh-huh. Dollar a day."

"Sure, but it's in Confederate money and ain't worth nothing."

Hanson gave Ragen a bleak look, and the trooper quickly became red in the face. "Look. Reb. I . . . I didn't mean anything. I was . . . I didn't think. I'm sorry. Okay?"

"Okay," Hanson said. He clapped Ragen on the shoulder and went to pick out the freshest looking meat from the pile of steaks they had cooked with their saddles and the last of any other burnable materials.

"You know," Thames mused aloud, "I used to think being rich and comfy meant getting to have steak for breakfast. Tell you the truth, boys, I'd be glad to settle for plain old army beans and bacon this morning . . . back at Camp Lune. No, t' hell with Lune. If I'm gonna imagine, I'd ruther imagine myself all the way back home in Michigan."

"That's where you're from, Chris? Michigan? What do you do there?"

"I'm a lumberjack. I can knock trees down quick as a crop farmer mowing barley with a scythe, I tell you." He wiped dry lips and took one of the steaks Hanson offered. "I used to live and work down in this here Arizona Territory, you know."

"Really?" Ragen asked with wide-eyed mock interest. He turned and winked at Berrenton and Hanson though.

"It's true, Al. I swear it. In fact, this is where I learned to cut trees."

"There's no trees here, Chris. I doubt there's a forest anywhere in this whole country."

"Now. But there sure was when I got here."

Gerd translated that, too, and judging by their reaction, the Swiss must never have heard that old chestnut before. They seemed to get quite a kick out of it.

"Eat up, boys," Berrenton said, "but mind you save your napkins. The laundry service is running a little behind schedule this week."

A half mile away, the Indians' smoke hung dark against the sky.

✛ 46 ✛

HEUER LET OUT a roar and spewed a torrent of German, and some of the Swiss ran to the handcarts while others grabbed their guns.

"Oh, shit," Berrenton groaned.

"Gone. Ist gone," Gerd bellowed.

"Christ, now what?" Thames asked.

"Somebody's helped himself to their gold again," Berrenton told them.

"They just got it back."

"Yes, and that one is safe on the ground over there. Now there's two other bags missing."

"Jeez, Corporal, how much of the stuff do they have?"

"Not so much that they can't keep track of it, I'm afraid."

"You give," the butcher shouted. "Give bock." The rest of them joined in along the same vein, all of them agitated, all of them shouting. One idiot, a guy named Anton, accidentally fired his rifle. Fortunately, the ball flew harmlessly toward the top of the cliff. The gunshot did nothing to ease the tension between the two groups.

Berrenton shoved his nose a couple inches beneath Gerd's chin and told him, in English, "You want to search our stuff again? Fine. Look all you damn want. Just don't bother us with any more of this crap. You know what I think, squarehead? I think it's one of your own damn people getting greedy and wanting a bigger cut than anybody else. That's what I think."

The words were obviously too fast and too many for Gerd to follow. He asked something in German, and Berrenton took a deep breath and tried again, slower this time and in German.

Heuer and Schwartman stood close by, taking this in. After some discussion that sounded suspiciously like an argument and which Berrenton did not see fit to translate for the others, the Swiss put their weapons down, and Karl and Gerd began a cursory inspection of the soldiers' blanket rolls. They acted like they did not expect to find anything and in the end did not.

"It's just a thought, Corporal," Hanson said, "but if I was interested in thieving some gold, I know where I'd hide it."

"And where would that be, Hanson?"

"Somewhere back by the dead. It stinks back there. Wouldn't anybody go poking around without pretty good reason."

Berrenton only shrugged, but Gerd obviously overheard and understood, at least in part. He said something to Karl, and the two of them walked to the back of the defile to continue their search for the missing gold.

Hanson winked at Berrenton and got a smile back in return. Wild-goose chases may not be productive, but they do give a body something to occupy himself with. And Hanson was entirely satisfied there was no stolen gold hidden in the burial area nor the abattoir because he and Gerd were the only people who had been back there since well before this latest theft must have occurred.

All of them, Swiss and American alike, had their attention returned to business by Ragen's call of, "Uh-oh, Corporal. Looks like somebody's kicked the anthill. They're stirring ag'in."

The soldiers hurried to the wall immediately. The Swiss lagged until Heuer saw and barked at the others to hit the defenses, too.

✤ 47 ✤

THE WHOLE CAMP full of Indians was mounted and moving, although with no discernible pattern or direction. Ragen's comment about a trod-upon anthill seemed entirely appropriate. The Indians appeared to be dashing about in willy-nilly disarray.

Anton, the Swiss with the nervous trigger finger, said something and pointed, everyone else quickly peering off in that direction, too.

"Looks like you got your wish, Chris."

"Is it too late t' change my mind?" Thames asked ruefully.

Far out on the right flank, another band of Indians could be seen coming in now.

"Anybody able to make out how many in this bunch?"

"A dozen. Maybe as many as fifteen," Hanson said.

"Ragen? You have good eyes."

"I'd say thirteen, Corporal. Could be fourteen. I'm not for sure."

"Plenty enough," Thames said.

"Stay ready, boys. The old crowd could be wanting to show off for these newcomers."

"You really know how to brighten a fella's day don't you, Corporal?"

"It's all part of command responsibility, Ragen. Keeping up squad morale, that's why I draw the big money."

"Could I ask you something, Corporal?"

"Sure. Go ahead."

"Is it true that you got those stripes tattooed on your arm?"

"That is a lie and a canard, Trooper. I had them tattooed on my ass."

"Thank you for clearing that up, Corporal."

"Anytime. Oops. I think we're about to have a visit. Check your caps, boys, and aim careful. We don't have a helluva lot of ammunition left, so mind you don't waste any of it."

The two groups of Indians converged. There was more milling and shouting and then, with a chilling chorus of screams that carried across the intervening quarter mile or so of desert, the unified body of savages charged straight at the thin line of white defenders.

✛ 48 ✛

DUST, GUNPOWDER SMOKE, the stench of decomposing bodies behind and the sharper stink of bowels being emptied in the aftermath of violent death in front. It was difficult to breathe.

The din was so loud the noise felt like a weight lying over them. Gunshots, screams of pain both human and equine, shrieks of rage, the crash of heavy bodies falling to the hard ground, and the clatter of spears and arrows ricocheting off stone. It was pandemonium, chaos, madness unending.

Hanson emptied his pistol and Joseph's, capped the sixth nipples in each gun and fired those. Put three rounds through the Sharps before the savages pressed so close and so hard there was no more time to load. He grabbed the barrel and used the buttstock as a club to kill a warrior whose horse had managed to jump the wall and enter the redoubt.

Ragen took the attack to the Indians, throwing down his empty weapons and scrambling in front of the wall. He kicked a teenage warrior in the cods and took the boy's tomahawk from him. With a sweep of the heavy blade, Ragen slashed the young warrior's throat open, very nearly severing the head from his body. Blood spurted five or six feet into the air before he fell.

For reasons Hanson could not know, Ragen bent over the warrior he had killed. Perhaps in the bloodlust that had come over him, he wanted to take the scalp. Whatever he intended, he had no time to complete the mission. A warrior on horseback ran a feathered spear into the small of Ragen's back.

Other Indians rushed to the fallen soldier and finished him with war clubs that had heads made of round stones the size of small cabbages. Ragen's skull collapsed at the first blow, and he surely would have been mercifully gone after that impact.

Hanson reloaded his revolver with his last four cartridges. He made a conscious effort to make his fingers slow and certain rather than risk dropping the tiny copper percussion caps without which the pistol would not discharge.

On the right, three warriors abandoned their horses and came over the wall, lashing out with clubs and tomahawks. Heuer went down. So did Schwartman.

Hanson ran to the right and with great care dispatched each of the savages. He had one round left in his Colt. His carbine's stock was broken. He picked up Ragen's Sharps and loaded it.

"I'm empty," Thames called.

Berrenton handed him a few cartridges, and Thames hurriedly reloaded.

There was . . . silence.

Hanson could scarcely believe it.

The quiet seemed empty, hollow.

The only thing he could hear was the receding thunder of hoofbeats as the attackers broke off the battle and retreated onto the desert floor.

"Jesus!" Hanson mumbled.

"Jesu!" He looked. Karl Bauer was standing there. The big Swiss had a gash on the side of his forehead that spread blood over the entire left side of his face and onto much of his torso, but the wound was not life threatening no matter how bad it appeared.

"That was close," Hanson said.

Karl made a comment in German. Hanson did not comprehend the words. He knew full well the sense of relief they intended.

"Corporal? Chris? Are you all right?"

"Yeah. I think so."

"Ask me tomorrow. If I'm still here then, I reckon I'm all right."

Wearily—the fight could not have lasted more than . . . what . . . fifteen or twenty minutes? . . . less?—Hanson laid the carbine down and shoved the almost empty Colt into his waistband.

He clambered over the wall and walked thirty-eight paces—he counted—toward the Indians. He stooped and with a grunt of effort lifted Al Ragen's body onto his shoulders. The damned savages were not the only ones who cared about their dead, damn them.

RAGEN HAD HAD eight pistol cartridges in his pouch when he died. Berrenton took them and divided them between Thames and Hanson, which meant Hanson had a full cylinder of five in the Colt plus—he opened his cartouche and fingered through the longtail paper cartridges there—another fourteen rounds for the much-slower-to-fire Sharps.

"He had sixteen rounds for the carbine," Berrenton said after he checked Ragen's supply.

"You're out of carbine ammo aren't you, Chris?" Hanson asked.

The trooper nodded.

"You and Chris split the Sharps ammo, Corporal. I still have some."

"If you're sure."

Berrenton, Hanson noticed, gave the lion's share of the cartridges to Thames.

The Swiss, it seemed, were almost as bad off for ammunition. They had a fairly decent amount of powder available but were short on cast lead balls and percussion caps. Berrenton asked; they had no mold to make more bullets.

But then there was nothing to burn to make a fire even

if they did want to cast balls, and no amount of powder or ball would be useful once they ran out of percussion caps. The Swiss were down to less than half a tin of caps.

"Got any extra revolver caps?" Berrenton asked. "Those should fit."

Thames and Hanson both handed over all the spares they possessed. But then with no more cartridges for the Colts, there was no need to save the caps for anything. Once the revolvers were emptied this time, there would be no reloading.

"Corporal."

"Yeah, Thames?"

"D'you think we can hold them off if they come again?"

Berrenton gave the trooper a wicked grin. "We'll slaughter the sons of bitches, Private."

Thames smiled. "Damn right we will, Corporal."

"Hanson, hand around some dried meat, will you? Then you can cut the throat of that Injun pony back there." Hanson had forgotten the horse that jumped the wall earlier. It stood now at the back of the notch. "Catch the blood. We'll get some liquid out of that. Use whatever stuff of the squareheads you like to collect it in. If they don't like that, tough. We all need the fluids.

"Thames, you get on the wall. My guess is they'll want to lick their wounds for a spell before they come again. *If* they come again. If we're lucky they'll figure they've taken enough of a beating and go away."

"Jeez, Corporal, do you think we're winning?"

"Close enough, kid. Now get on with it. You've got guard duty until I relieve you."

"Yes, Corporal."

"Right," Hanson said crisply. He bent to the tasks he was assigned. Berrenton went over to confer with the four Swiss who remained.

✦ 50 ✦

"R^{EB.}"

"Yeah, Chris?"

"Are you scared to die?"

"Yes."

"You ain't lying to me, are you? Just to make me feel better, like?"

"No, I'm not lying to you, Chris. I'm scared to die. So is Jesse, I'm sure. Know what I'm more scared of? I'm more scared of failing you and Jesse than I am of dying. And that's the truth."

Thames smiled. "Yeah."

Hanson leaned against the wall, pistol secured in the issue holster and Sharps laid close to hand. He did not expect another attack so soon and in fact was pleasantly comfortable.

The direct heat of the sun had abated as the afternoon waned, and right now the galls in his armpits and groin were mildly tender but not actively painful. His belly was full, and even his thirst satiated thanks to the brown and white Indian pony.

And he was alive.

There was quite a lot to be said for that, too.

"You know what I been thinking about?" Thames asked.

"Mm?"

"That gold. Who do you think stole it?"

Hanson shrugged. "Does it matter?"

"No, I expect not. I was just wondering."

The truth was that Hanson was fairly sure he knew who the thief was. It pretty much had to be Berrenton. He was the only one of the soldiers who spent any time in the Swiss part of the compound. Ragen had scarcely left the wall. Chris hadn't taken it or he would not have brought the subject up. Besides, Thames seemed guileless and decent. Hanson was willing to trust his feelings on that score.

Which left Berrenton.

And a man is not necessarily a model of virtue just because he proves himself to be a warrior and a leader of men. In fact, the direct opposite would often be true. So Berrenton was in charge of ferreting out the criminal for the crime he himself committed. Hanson rather liked the absurdity of that. And it was not, after all, his gold that was missing.

"You know what I'm gonna do if we get out of here?" Thames asked.

"Mm."

"I'm gonna walk away from this man's army. Just . . . walk clean away."

"Where to?"

"California, I think. It's right over there, right?" He nodded toward the west.

"Yes, I expect that it is."

"Right. And when those Injuns leave, I'm gonna go there."

"What about the squad?"

"Us three, that's all that's left of the squad, Reb. You think the corporal will try an' stop me from going?"

"No, I wouldn't think so." If Hanson's guess about Berrenton was correct, he was betting the corporal would be on his way to California right along with Chris.

And as for himself . . . He'd given his parole. His feeling right now was that he had met the conditions of that parole honorably enough.

Maybe he would go to California, too.

Hanson began to laugh very softly to himself.

Thames noticed. "What's so funny?"

"Oh, I was just thinking about something, that's all." It would not be fair of him to tell Thames what it was that he found so amusing.

Hope and a belief in one's own immortality, though, was what he found to be so funny.

Because, assurances to Thames aside, none of them was likely to survive this encounter. Not the squad and not the Swiss miners, either.

Unless the Indians became bored with this fight and went off to do something else instead, not a one of them was apt to live more than . . . call it tomorrow sundown at the latest, he thought.

It was late enough in the day now that they probably would not come again this afternoon.

But come dawn tomorrow . . . with so few defenders and practically no ammunition, they would not be able to survive another assault like that last one.

One more good charge, and they were finished, every last one of them.

That seemed one helluva pity. There had been a time when he would gladly have died—gloriously, to be sure— for the South. Then another time when, knowing there was no damned glory to be found in war, he would have been not glad but certainly willing to die for the future of the South that he so truly and passionately loved. There never once was a time when he could consider himself willing to die for the perfidious Union. To serve, yes, but not to die.

And now . . . it seemed he was fated to die wearing this uniform of blue after all.

Lordy, he wished he had his own proud gray to wear when he faced the Maker.

"Reb."

"Yes, Chris?"

"Am I bothering you with all my questions?"

Hanson smiled. "No, Chris. You ask anything you like." He laughed softly. "I'm not going anywhere, you know."

Thames smiled, too. "Yeah, well I was wondering . . ."

✣ 51 ✣

THE INDIANS WERE at it again. They built a huge fire and were dancing and yelping around it like the crazy damned savages they were.

"You know what I think?" Hanson offered. "I think this fight is some kind of ... I don't know ... ceremonial thing with them. Something on that order anyhow. You know the way they keep sending young boys armed with the feathered sticks? I think this must be some rite of passage or proof of manhood. Like that. And that's why all the dancing and the new groups coming in and the boys with the sticks." He frowned. "Bet it's why they won't quit and leave us the hell alone despite the casualties, too."

"We've killed a lot of them," Thames said.

Berrenton contributed to the conversation for the first time since sundown. "I always heard Indians wouldn't press a long, hard fight. These ones sure are." He spat. "You could be right, Hanson. Could even be some kind of religious thing with them, I suppose."

"Where the hell is a Methodist preacher when you need one," Hanson said with a smile. "We need to convert these boys. Show them the error of their ways."

"Feel free if you want to, Hanson. Walk right out there

and give them a sermon on how they oughta act."

"I may just do that, Corporal. Quick as I get my sermon thought out. Got any writing paper and ink so I can get it all written down?"

"I'll see what I can find for you, Hanson. That's a promise."

"Thank you, Corporal."

Over to the right there was a loud, rasping buzz. One of the Swiss was snoring fit to drown out a steam engine's hiss and puff.

"You think they'll come at dawn, Hanson?" Thames asked for probably the twelfth time.

"I think I've given up trying to guess what these Indians are up to, Chris. The only thing I know for sure is that they'll do whatever they damn please. It's up to us to still be standing here after they've gone and done it."

"You think we can hold them off? Really?"

"Yes, I do, Chris. Yes, I surely do," he lied with a smile.

"But do you think—"

There was a roar of fury and a loud thump from the direction of the Swiss. Hanson and Thames both crouched and spun, ready to meet a threat. This time, though, the threat was not directed toward them.

Karl and a man named Jean-Luc were rolling around on the ground like a pair of cats going at each other. It took Hanson a moment to realize that the two Swiss had Jesse Berrenton underneath them and were pummeling him hard and heavy.

"Hey! Stop that." Thames started to rush to the corporal's rescue, but Hanson grabbed the trooper by the shoulder and held him back. "Let me go, Reb. Those foreign sons of bitches are beating up on the corporal."

"This is between him and them, Chris. Leave them be."

"But—"

"Jesse is the one who's been sneaking bags out of the gold cart, Chris."

"No!"

"I haven't seen him do it. But I'm pretty sure it's so."

"But they'll kill him," Thames wailed. There was real fear in his voice. Thames was afraid of finding himself facing the hostiles without a leader to guide him, Hanson realized.

"No, they won't. Not as long as those Indians are out there. We need every gun. That includes Jesse."

Anton joined into the melee, helping pin Berrenton to the ground while Gerd came warily toward Hanson and Thames. "He taken our golt."

Hanson nodded. "Yes, I think he did."

"May be ve kill him."

"No," Hanson said flatly. "You will not."

"You vould stop us?"

Hanson nodded. "I would stop you."

"How you do?"

Hanson unfastened the flap over his holster, exposing the grips of the .44 Colt. He did not draw the pistol. But then he did not think he would have to. He doubted that the Swiss wanted Berrenton dead any more than he did. And they were certainly entitled to some threats and bluster.

Gerd stared hard at Hanson for a moment as if trying to assess whether the soldier meant what he said. After a moment he turned and barked something in German. Karl stood. Jean-Luc and Anton picked up a rather limp corporal by the arms, holding him like a scarecrow fallen from its stake.

"Bassards," the corporal mumbled. Which was good. It meant he was alive and likely would stay that way for the time being, probably until the Indians took a hand and not the Swiss.

"Shut up, Jesse. You deserve it."

"You're bad as 'em, you damn Johnny Reb."

"Yes, but we need you, and you need us. Now shut up before they decide to beat on you some more, will you?"

Berrenton shut up.

"Let me make a suggestion, Jesse. Give them back what you stole earlier. Where do you have it hidden?"

"Go t'hell."

"In due time I probably will. But that's another story, isn't it? Now would you please just give the damned gold back. You can't spend it here anyway."

"Been poor all m' damn life," Berrenton grumbled.

"Better to live poor than die rich. Now give it back so we can pay attention to business."

Berrenton struggled upright. He was weak and swaying but able to support himself. Gerd said something, and Anton and Jean-Luc stepped aside.

"Get it, Jesse. Please."

The corporal walked with exaggerated care to the bedroll that had belonged to Private Joseph. He shook out the blanket and three bags of gold fell to the ground, prompting another spate of anger from the Swiss who apparently hadn't realized how much was taken from them.

"I was gonna share with you an' Thames," the corporal growled as if that somehow excused the thievery.

"And I believe you, too," Hanson said.

Chris Thames turned his back in disgust.

Come daybreak though, Hanson was sure, Thames would obey Berrenton as unquestioningly as ever. That was simply the nature of soldiering, and Thames was a soldier serving in the face of an enemy.

The Swiss rushed to reclaim their property, giving dark looks to all the Americans.

"Gerd."

"Ja?"

"You boys might as well take the watch now. It's only

a little early, and I doubt any of you will be going back to sleep real soon."

"Ja. Ve do." He said something to the others, and they picked up their weapons and went to the wall. All of them except Karl, who perched on one of the gold cart's wheels with his attention on the soldiers rather than the wall.

"All right," Hanson said. "The excitement is over for tonight. Let's see if we can't get some sleep." He grunted. "Just could be that we'll need it come tomorrow."

IN THE COLD light of dawn it was children who came again, not warriors. Two of them mounted on short, potbellied ponies, each of them carrying only one of those feathered sticks. Neither boy looked more than ten or eleven years old. They didn't have painted faces or torsos like the grown-ups, nor were their horses decorated with the hands and dots and swirls of color that the adults used.

They were children who had not earned the right to those outward symbols, Hanson guessed. Yet.

Perhaps that was what this was all about, proving that they were brave enough to join the warriors in actual fighting.

"Stand fast but don't fire," he ordered in a crisp, no-nonsense voice. Then felt his cheeks go warm with embarrassment when he remembered he had no business giving orders here.

But then, Jesse Berrenton was in no condition to be giving orders right now either. The corporal stood at the wall but with his head down and attention far from the moment. Likely he was hurting pretty badly.

And one of the Swiss—this time it was Anton—continued to sit on the handcart, guarding their damned gold even though he might well be needed on the wall.

The two boys separated and came dashing past one at a time. Hanson stood where he was. So did Chris Thames. The boy leaned low over the withers of his pony and tapped first Hanson and then Chris with the feathered end of his stick before he raced on by.

"Here comes the other one. Don't shoot the little bastard," Hanson cautioned.

This one was a real show-off. He charged to a point directly in front of the wall and about five yards distant, stopped his pony there, and shrieked taunts and curses at the defenders. Spun the animal twice around and flung his stick like a spear, then came nearer to the wall and leaned out to touch Chris on the head with his fingertips.

Hanson was hoping the kid would come to him next as the other had just done. Try that trick one more time, and Hanson would have himself a prisoner. See if the savages were in a mood to negotiate a trade.

And if that made the sons of bitches mad, so what. They couldn't get much worse than they were right now, he thought, and it just might persuade them to quit playing this ugly game and go hunt buffalo. Or whatever it was Indians hunted around here. Popular misconception had them hunting buffalo all the damned time, but the simple truth was that Hanson hadn't seen one lousy buffalo since he came out here with the Yankee army. For that matter, hadn't ever seen one before that time either, there not being a whole hell of a lot of buffalo in the woods where he grew up.

In any event, the smart-aleck Indian boy touched Chris with his bare hand, then turned his pony and put the heels to it, sending the stocky little horse into a hard run straight from the redoubt to the Indian camp far to the front.

"You should've shot 'im," Berrenton grumbled.

"If you wanted him shot, Jesse, you could've done it yourself," Hanson returned.

The corporal did not respond. And in truth, Hanson

doubted that he could have shot the kid after all. Even at point-blank range. He looked awfully shaky. As soon as the Indian boys were back with their own and no threat to the whites, Berrenton turned and slumped to the ground at the base of the wall.

Hanson found himself hoping the adult savages would take some time to celebrate with those boys before they attacked again. It would be bad enough trying to defend with only seven guns, all the worse with but five, which was what they would have if neither Jesse Berrenton nor Anton stood to the wall.

"Oh, shit," Chris blurted, wiping their little internal problems completely out of Hanson's thoughts.

Out on the desert the Indians were all mounted now and were massing in plain sight.

There must have been upwards of seventy or eighty of them.

"Anton! Jesse!" Hanson pointed to the wall. He did not need any German to get that message across.

Gerd said something, too, and Anton grabbed the shotgun and hurried to join the line of defenders. Berrenton struggled upright, but Hanson didn't know how much good the corporal would be. But then anything would help at this point.

"Hanson."

"Yeah, Chris?"

"Do you really and truly think—"

"I think we can, Chris. I think we can do it. Just take your time and aim nice and deliberate. We can't be wasting any ammunition here."

"Yes, sir." Thames did not seem to realize that he'd responded as if Hanson were an officer But then neither did Jesse Berrenton, so there was no harm done, no authority having been undermined.

The Indians began to yelp and howl, and the milling of

so many hoofs lifted a thick cloud of dust into the still morning air.

"They're coming now. Check your pieces and make ready," Hanson barked.

✢ 53 ✢

"HOLD YOUR FIRE. Hold fire, dammit!"
Gerd shot a questioning look at Hanson and hesitated for a moment, then repeated the order in German.

"Oh, Jesus," Thames whispered. "Are you sure?"

Hanson did not take time to answer. He was paying attention to the Indians, who were not acting like they did in a charge. This rush was more like one of those feathered stick things except from longer range. The horde of savages swept across the front at a distance of sixty or seventy yards, moving fast from left to right and all of them bunched tight together.

"Hold fire. This isn't . . . I don't know what this is. But let's see." He was saying it more for his own benefit than Chris Thames's. And Chris would surely be the only one listening to him. Except for Gerd, the Swiss couldn't understand him, and Jesse Berrenton was standing upright but appeared to be only half conscious. "Hold now . . . hold."

The Indians raced past in a body, a pack of young boys at the very front—all of the kids who'd come in with the sticks over the past few days? Hanson thought perhaps so—and the painted warriors trailing.

They thundered by and turned. Turned not toward the

wall to attack but out onto the desert again, quickly disappearing into the almost imperceptible rise and fall of the terrain.

They left behind only dust that hung in the air like smoke.

"You know what I noticed?" Thames asked. "Some o' those horses was packing dead Injuns. I'd swear they was. Bodies wrapped in something and tied over the backs of the horses."

"That's what I thought they were, too."

"You don't think—"

"We couldn't be so lucky," Hanson told him.

"Maybe not, but it sure-God looks that way. D'you think maybe they finished what they come here for? Something about those kids with the sticks? An' now they've gone off again?"

"I think . . . Lordy, Chris, I don't want to even think such a thing lest I jinx the possibility."

Thames turned to Hanson with a huge grin and a shout of sheer joy. "We done it, Reb. We really done it."

And even though it was far too much to think, much less to really hope . . . Hanson had to concede that it really did look that way.

He placed his carbine onto the wall beside Thames and added his cartridge pouch. "Stay here," he said. "I'm going to go see what's out there."

"Don't . . . you can't leave us here, sir. Please."

"I'll be back. I promise." He grinned and added, "Unless the Indians are still out there, that is. But I won't leave you alone."

"Yes, sir."

Hanson clambered over the wall and stood there for a moment.

The decent thing, he supposed, would be to leave his pistol with Thames, too. Just in case it was needed by the defenders. If the savages were still there, one Colt revolver would be no protection from them.

On the other hand, if he did see them, Trooper Joseph's form of escape would be the best way out. He certainly did not want to suffer the agonies that Vickers had. No, he would keep the pistol.

He took a moment to lift his hat and let a little fresh air reach his scalp, then took a deep breath and began walking out onto the desert toward the dry wash where they'd stopped to mount their own charge those long days past.

✛ 54 ✛

HE COULDN'T STOP grinning. None of them could. They kept slapping each other on the back and congratulating themselves and practically soaring six feet off the ground with joy and relief and an exhilarating sense of being alive.

"My God, Reb, my God," Thames kept saying.

Even Jesse Berrenton looked like he was feeling better. A little.

The Swiss were babbling and screaming as loud as the Indians had. Hanson could not help thinking that the cart of gold would look even nicer split four ways than twelve. But that was an unkind thought, and he kept it to himself. The Swiss had fought as valiantly as anyone.

"You should see it out there," Hanson said. "It's unbelievable, the mess they left behind. They're filthy sons of bitches, and that's a fact. They don't bother to dig latrines, just take a dump right on the ground. It stinks almost as bad where they were camped as it does here." He shook his head and frowned.

"How about the dead ones? Could you tell how many we killed? Or did they take all of them with them when they left?"

"There's not a single body out there. Nor much of anything else either. Some fire rings and cold ashes. Bunch of crap on the ground. Gnawed bones and some scraps of bloody rags. That's about it."

"Oh man, though. Oh man. I thought sure we was going under," Thames said. "I didn't think there was any way we'd get out of this."

Hanson shrugged. "Warfare is a crazy business, Chris. I guess those Indians got done with the manhood rites . . . or whatever it was they were doing . . . and decided enough of them had died; they didn't want to fight anymore. To tell the truth, I've seen the same sort of thing with civilized troops. Guys fight all day long, then come evening it's like everybody decides they've fought enough. They quit shooting and no amount of cajoling will get them to start up again. Not that same day anyhow. I've seen that, I think, two different times back East."

"Really? Our boys did that?"

"Uh-huh. So did ours."

"I think . . . sometimes it's hard to think of you as being the enemy, Hanson. Real hard."

"I'll take that as a compliment, Chris."

"Yeah. You do that. I mean it, too."

They stood there grinning at each other, lighthearted and free. Having a future to look toward again. It was a wonderful feeling.

Gerd approached them, ignoring the corporal. "You go fort now, ja?"

"Yes, I expect that we will. And you? Where will your people go?"

"Calipornia," Gerd said. "Him." He hooked a thumb toward Berrenton. "Dat t'ief. You tell sojer boss he t'ief, ja?"

"No, Gerd, it isn't my place to do that. He is my corporal, and I'll not be disloyal to him. If you want Jesse charged with anything, you come with us to Camp Lune and tell your story to the lieutenant. I will tell the truth if there is an inquiry. I'm sure Chris will, too. But I won't initiate anything. That you will have to do for yourselves."

Gerd turned and spoke briefly with the other Swiss. Then he said, "To 'ell wit you dem sojers. We go Calipornia. Dem all you."

Hanson shrugged. "Whatever you want, squarehead. It doesn't make any nevermind to me."

Gerd and Karl took hold of the handles of their carts while Anton and Jean-Luc hurriedly cast aside enough of the wall stones to allow the handcarts to be dragged outside.

"Gerd."

"Ja?"

"Wait."

"Ja?"

"I am commandeering that handcart. Not the one with the gold. That is yours. But I need that other cart. The corporal is in no condition to walk all the way back to camp after what you people did to him last night. I'm taking your cart so we can use it for an ambulance."

"You don' take nutting, dem you."

"Mister, you are on American soil here, and I am an American soldier. I am taking that cart. Chris, I intend to appropriate the cart. If those civilians try to stop me, I want you to shoot them."

Thames's eyes went wide. But he stepped half a pace back and drew his Colt.

"Make up your mind what you want to do, Gerd. If the cart means that much to you, you are welcome to accompany it to Camp Lune. I will return it to you there. Not before."

The Swiss spoke to his companions. Karl and Anton gave Hanson glares that were positively murderous. But they stepped away from the cart that held their clothing and other gear and took up only the one that contained their gold.

The four Swiss muscled the heavily laden cart over what remained of the wall and started south without a backward glance or a word of parting.

But then, despite the experiences the two groups shared, it was never friendship that held them together.

"Come along, Chris. Let's put the corporal in that cart and get out of here."

"We're going back to Camp Lune?"

"Uh-huh. Soon as we've gotten some water. We'll need that."

Thames looked confused. "There's no water here, Hanson."

"Yes, there is. Down that way." He nodded in the direction the Swiss were moving. "Has to be. And fairly close, too. Those Indians and their horses haven't been going without water all this time, and I've noticed dust rising to and from the south a couple times each day. There has to be water there. Probably somewhere along the base of this mesa is what I'd guess. It's going to be a slow walk back to Lune, so we'll gather up all the canteens and put them in the cart with the corporal. And then, my young friend, we three will get the hell out of here."

"Yes sir, Reb." Thames hurried to grab up the long-empty canteens while Hanson assisted Berrenton into the remaining handcart.

They could not get away from this terrible place quickly enough to suit him.

THE SWISS HAD found the water, too. That was not surprising, because after the many trips the Indians made to it there was a beaten path that a blind hog could have followed.

The water was in a stone dish or basin that was a good ten by fifteen feet in size, tucked close against the base of the mesa and fed by a thin trickle that seeped out of the rock a half dozen feet up the cliffside. Hanson could not see how deep the pool was, but there was enough water in it to have satisfied the needs of the Indians and all their horses.

The Swiss were still there when the soldiers arrived. By common consent, the Swiss moved to one side of the basin and the Americans approached it on the other. The two groups eyed each other but did not speak or otherwise acknowledge the others' existence.

Water. God! It was magnificent.

Hanson drank until he thought his belly would burst, then took a full canteen and walked a few paces away from the basin. He unbuttoned his shirt and dropped it to his waist so he could pour cool, cleansing water over his head and into his armpits. The heat galls felt immediately better. The relief would not last long. He knew that. But it was wonderful while it did.

When he was done with that, he dropped his britches and did the same for the sores in his groin. Then he poured what was left in his hat and swished it around. The evaporation process would keep his head cool for the next hour if he was lucky.

He went back to the basin, refilled the canteen, and then did it all again.

Thames was grinning, and even Berrenton acted like he was beginning to feel better once he had his belly filled.

Hanson passed around the dried horsemeat they had piled into the handcart along with the corporal. The Swiss had not thought to bring any. Their attention had been solely on the gold when they hurriedly left the redoubt. Now perhaps they were regretting that. Hanson ignored their pointed stares and kept the rest of the supplies for his own people.

The Swiss made a few choice comments in German— best that he did not know what those comments were, Hanson was sure—then sent a few dark looks toward the Americans and walked off toward the south again, dragging the gold cart with them.

They were welcome to it, Hanson thought. He and Thames and Berrenton still had their lives. And that was much, much more than he expected to have right now.

"There's some deadwood over there," Thames was saying, "and I have a burning glass here if you want to start a fire an' cook some o' this meat."

"That's probably a good idea, Chris. We can stay here for a day or two. Let the corporal get to feeling better before we start back. We can—"

He stopped speaking. Probably his heart stopped, too. The interruption was caused by a hideous outpouring of shrieks and whoops and a thunder of hoofs as a dozen Indians came charging out of a shallow swale.

They targeted the Swiss, who were exposed on bare ground with nowhere to hide and no way to run.

The Swiss seemed paralyzed with shock and horror. Only one of them—Hanson could not see who—managed to get off a shot.

The Indians swarmed over them. Shooting arrows. Stabbing with spears. Smashing with the stone war clubs.

It was over within seconds, but even then the Indians did not let up. They leaped from their ponies and stood over their victims stabbing and hacking with knives and clubs and spear points until the four miners were reduced to scraps of bloody meat.

Thames threw up. Hanson did not blame him. The murders took place not a hundred yards distant, and they could see the ferocity of the savages all too clearly.

"Into the rocks," Hanson snapped. "Jesse, can you walk? No? C'mon, Chris. Help me drag him up there. Bring whatever canteens you can carry, too."

Hanson picked up a stack of the dried meat and two canteens, then took Berrenton by one arm while Chris took the other. They dragged the corporal between them, rushing into the protection of a pair of boulders that lay on the south side of the water basin.

Nearby, the Indians grew tired of desecrating the corpses of the Swiss. They mounted their ponies and set up a howling again, brandishing their weapons and shouting taunts.

This time it was the three blue-clad soldiers whose blood they wanted.

"Well, damn," Hanson grumbled.

"Say, Reb? What d'you think?"

Hanson barked a coldly humorless laugh. "Oh hell, Chris. There's not but thirteen or fourteen of the devils. I say we have them outnumbered."

"That's what I thought, too."

"You ready, Jesse?"

"Uh."

He didn't sound ready. Not that it mattered now.

The Indians' screaming became all the more bloodcurdling, and as one, the riders broke into a hard run straight at the soldiers.

56

HANSON DID NOT wait for them to close on the soldiers' position. He raised his carbine and took aim on the breastbone of the leading rider. The Sharps spat flame, and the Indian dropped under the hoofs of the riders coming close behind him.

The rest of the savages swerved aside, splitting into two halves with one breaking left and the other right.

Thames and Berrenton both fired, too, while Hanson quickly reloaded, but he did not see any hits. Certainly no more Indians were unhorsed.

"Bastards," he hissed. "They knew we had to come to water. They were waiting for us to all arrive."

"Three of us left now," Thames said.

"Two and a half," Hanson corrected.

"You go t' hell," Berrenton hissed.

Hanson laughed. "Good for you, Jesse."

"Bastard."

Hanson was not sure if Berrenton was referring to the Indians or to him. "Hey, Jesse."

"What do you want now, dammit?"

"I still think you're one hell of a soldier."

"Yeah, well, thanks for standing up for me with those squareheads."

"You're sounding better."

"I'm feeling better. You know what I think? I think if we can hold them off for another charge or maybe two, they'll give up and leave us be. They aren't doing that ceremony stuff now, and there's no young ones to take to school. Now it's just us and them. And not so damn many of them, either. I think we can still make it out of this."

"All right. How're you fixed for ammunition?"

"I got seven cartridges left, I think."

"Chris?"

"Four in my pistol. Eight for the carbine, I think."

"Like I said . . . we got them outnumbered. Should we go surround them now or wait for them to come to us?"

"I'm still a little tired," Berrenton said. "Let's let them do the hard part an' come to us."

"Bastards," Hanson said without rancor, it being a soldier's God-given right to bellyache if he wanted to.

Out in front of them they could hear the Indians working themselves into a frenzy again.

"I think we're about to have company," Hanson said. "This time let's pour it on them just as hot and heavy as we can. Make them think twice about coming for a third time." If, he thought silently to himself, they could break the second charge. If!

"They're coming," Thames said. "I see them."

All three drew their hammers back to full cock.

They waited.

57

FLAME AND SMOKE engulfed the tiny defensive enclave as all three fired as fast as they could load and aim. At least four of the Indians fell, the remaining eight or nine coming within twenty feet of the boulders before their charge broke and they whirled away.

"Close," Thames said in a quavering voice. "That was close."

"Wasn't it just. Are you okay?"

"I think so. Yeah."

"Jesse?"

There was no answer.

Hanson looked in his direction. "Damn!"

Berrenton was sprawled on his back, eyes sightlessly turned to the sky and the feathered shaft of an arrow protruding from the base of his neck. The front of his uniform was saturated with blood that was dark against the blue wool.

"Get his guns and ammunition, Chris."

"You think they'll come again?"

"I would if I were them. But I sure hope they won't."

Thames shivered despite the heat of the day. Then he

bent to gather Berrenton's carbine and revolver and ammunition pouches.

It was not yet noon on what Hanson calculated to be the last day of his life.

"Bastards," he said again.

✢ 58 ✢

"I GOT ONE, Reb; I got me another one." Thames fired, hurried to reload, and fired again.

The Indians were practically close enough to reach out and touch.

Thames drew his revolver and stood, coolly firing as if on the practice range. He brought down at least one Indian before two arrows and a thrown spear pierced his body and he fell.

Dust enveloped him as the Indian ponies' hoofs churned the soil.

Arrows clattered against the rocks.

And then they were gone, the third charge broken against the rock of Chris Thames's courage.

"You did good, boy, damnyankee or not," Hanson whispered.

He felt immeasurably alone and vulnerable there with only two dead men for company.

There had been more Indians, not fewer, in this last charge. Some of the others must have heard the shooting and returned to join in on the fun.

"Bastards," he said aloud.

He reached into his cartridge pouch and blanched, a sickly empty feeling in the pit of his stomach when searching fingers could find no more of the fat little paper sausages filled with gunpowder and lead.

The third charge exhausted his ammunition.

Quickly he knee-walked over to Thames's body, but his pouch, too, was empty. And they had stripped the corporal of his last rounds after the second Indian charge.

Hanson grabbed Thames's carbine. Empty.

He picked up the Colt that Chris held in his last moments. The revolver was empty.

Hanson checked his own .44. It, too, was empty.

He hadn't saved the last cartridge for himself. He probably should have.

If the Indians came again . . . when the Indians came again . . .

He stood, rage overcoming reason. Stepped out from behind the boulders where the three of them had taken refuge.

In front of him eighty or ninety yards the Indians were massing for another attack, their ponies as excited as the savages who rode them.

Hanson turned, dropped his trousers and bent over.

He could hear the Indians howl.

"Come get me, you sons of bitches, but you aren't going to take me alive, damn you!"

With his fist and right arm he made a universal gesture of contempt, then picked up his empty carbine and turned it to use the butt as a club.

He started a quick and deliberate march toward the twenty or so Indians who now stopped their horses from milling and sat watching the white man come at them with only a club in his hands.

One of the savages stepped his horse forward. Stopped and shrieked something into the still, late-morning air. Turned and yammered something at the others.

The Indian thumped his pony's ribs, and the horse sprang forward.

THE INDIAN YANKED his pony to a sliding stop practically in Hanson's face. The Indian was a large man, stout of body, with gray streaking his oily hair. His face and upper body were streaked with paint and mud in patterns that were marred where running sweat partially washed them away.

Hanson hefted his makeshift club and waited for the Indian to mount an arrow on his bowstring and put an end to it. Hanson's head was held high and there was defiance in his eyes. He glared up at the mounted warrior, who grunted softly and turned his horse so the animal's right side was presented.

The Indian took his bow by the lower end and reached out with the tuft of feathers that decorated the tip of the weapon.

He rapped Hanson hard on the right shoulder.

Hanson stepped forward and tried to smash the Indian's knee with a butt stroke.

The pony shied away, the Indian holding his balance effortlessly, even though he rode bareback.

Before Hanson could attempt again to strike, the Indian snatched the pony's head around and put it into a run toward the others.

The savages conferred, and a moment later a second warrior, this one younger but just as ugly, came forward. This one charged straight at Hanson. The shoulder of his pony hit Hanson in the chest and he went sprawling. He lost his grip on the Sharps but scrambled on hands and knees to recover it and jump to his feet again. Before he could strike with the empty carbine, the Indian hit him with his bow, this time on the left shoulder.

The Indian cantered back to the others while a third came out.

This time Hanson stood and waited. He held the Sharps ready but did not try to strike.

The Indian swept past, slashing Hanson across the back with the hard flat of his bow.

A fourth stopped in front of Hanson and sat there staring for a moment. The warrior's eyes were cold. Yet, inexplicably, he only touched Hanson on the forehead with the sticky, blood-crusted ball of a war club that must all too recently have been used on the skulls of one or more of the Swiss miners.

Hanson glared back at him.

The Indian wheeled around and raced away.

No more of the riders offered to detach themselves from the pack to engage in this strange behavior of wanting to touch a live enemy without killing him.

Hanson steeled himself for what was to come.

Without warning, the Indians began to move again, their ponies spinning around and breaking into a trot.

Away. Off toward the north.

Hanson's knees were watery, and he began to tremble.

The Indians lifted their mounts to a lope, and they were gone from sight within moments.

Hanson was having difficulty seeing. His vision was as watery as his legs. He tried to take a step only to collapse, unable to walk or think or understand.

Later there would be time enough to bury the dead as

best he could and collect some water and dried meat.

And that handcart bearing the dead men's gold.

Later. California would still be there later.

Now he only wanted to lie in the sun with tears coursing over his cheeks.

Later.

From Spur Award-winning author
FRANK RODERUS

Dead Man's Journey	0-425-18554-0
Winter Kill	0-425-18099-9
Left to Die	0-425-17637-1
Outlaw with a Star	0-425-16817-4

"Frank Roderus writes a lean, tough book."
—Douglas Hirt

"Frank Roderus makes the West seem so real, you'd swear he'd been there himself long ago." —Jory Sherman

Available wherever books are sold or to order call 1-800-788-6262